CW00558215

A DEATH
at
Bay View
HOTEL

BOOKS BY EMMA JAMESON

Jemima Jago Mystery Series

A Death at Seascape House

A Death at Candlewick Castle

A Death at Silversmith Bay

A Death at Neptune Cove

Dr. Benjamin Bones Mystery Series

Bones in the Blackout

Bones at the Manor House

Bones Takes a Holiday

Bones Buried Deep

Lord and Lady Hetheridge Mystery Series

Ice Blue

Blue Murder

Something Blue

Black and Blue

Blue Blooded

Blue Christmas

Untrue Blue

A DEATH
at
Bay View
HOTEL

EMMA JAMESON

bookouture

Published by Bookouture in 2023

An imprint of Storyfire Ltd.
Carmelite House
50 Victoria Embankment
London EC4Y 0DZ

www.bookouture.com

Copyright © Emma Jameson, 2023

Emma Jameson has asserted her right to be identified
as the author of this work.

All rights reserved. No part of this publication may be reproduced, stored in
any retrieval system, or transmitted, in any form or by any means, electronic,
mechanical, photocopying, recording or otherwise, without the prior written
permission of the publishers.

ISBN: 978-1-83790-192-0
eBook ISBN: 978-1-83790-191-3

This book is a work of fiction. Names, characters, businesses, organizations,
places and events other than those clearly in the public domain, are either
the product of the author's imagination or are used fictitiously. Any
resemblance to actual persons, living or dead, events or locales is entirely
coincidental.

For Donna

1

DEADLY DELIGHT

Jem arrived in Ballroom A of the Bay View Hotel to find her friend Pauley Gwyn already up on the dais, welcoming only fifty people to the Isles of Scilly's 17th Annual Valentine's Bake Off. It was a sad comedown for an event that usually drew crowds that were standing room only.

By early February, Jem's fellow islanders were anxious for spring and eager to participate in something. Some just wanted a day out, booking a ferry to St. Martin's for sweets and eats. Others, feeling the pinch of winter heating bills, came as vendors, hoping to sell anything from homemade chutney to knitted caps. This year's venue had ratcheted up the excitement because the Bay View Hotel was new and luxurious. Located on the westernmost tip of St. Martin's and overlooking the Celtic Sea, it was tastefully grand, inside and out. With meteorologists promising that Storm Veronica would close out the winter with a bang, the islanders had been eager to soak up Bay View's ambience before bad weather shuttered every business. But the storm had made a surprise appearance, slamming into St. Martin's two days early.

If Ballroom A seemed a bit sad despite its dusty rose and silver appointments, not to mention Pauley's Valentine-themed balloons and banners, then Ballroom B next door looked like purgatory. Jem, who'd peeked inside on her way to the main event, had found the designated vendors space was mostly empty tables. Although dozens of local artisans, cooks, and vintners had signed up, they'd been unwilling or unable to risk the passage to St. Martin's. Lucky them. Jem and her fellow early birds were now stuck at the Bay View. Alongside a handful of contestants, the hotel staff, and about fifty stranded hotel guests, most of whom were in no mood to buy Isles of Scilly souvenirs.

At least we're inside, safe and dry, Jem thought. Automatically, she checked her mobile, hoping against hope that satellite coverage had returned. Of course, it hadn't. Rain was pounding down on the islands, beating a fierce rhythm on the hotel roof. Fortunately, the Bay View had generator power, keeping the lights and heat on. As for the Annual Valentine's Day Bake Off, the committee could have been forgiven for calling the whole thing off. But only one committee representative had made it to St. Martin's—this year's chair, Pauley Gwyn, and Gwyns didn't give up.

Sometimes I wish she would, Jem thought, surreptitiously glancing around a roomful of grim faces. *Talk about a tough crowd.*

At a destination like the Bay View, guests checked in and out most days. That made room for a new crop of holidaymakers who could reasonably be expected to enjoy some local color and an opportunity to pick up some trinkets. The Bake Off was scheduled to take advantage of those fresh-faced newcomers. But thanks to Storm Veronica, ferry service was canceled, and helicopters were grounded.

Meaning none of the Bay View's incoming guests had arrived, and none of the departing crowd had left.

Now the hotel was populated only by staff and by stranded travelers who'd expected to be halfway home by now. Worse, all the pleasant wireless-based activities of daily life—satellite TV, mobile phones, laptops—were limited or kaput. Even going for a walk was out. Although it was two o'clock in the afternoon, the skies were dark, and the winds were fierce. Anyone trying to take a gander at the huge waves would be drenched by rain and bent over by gales, if not blown right off their feet.

That's why most of them are here, daring Pauley to entertain them, Jem thought. Judging by body language—folded arms, tight lips, jutting chins—nothing would cheer up these thwarted travelers short of an absolute disaster.

Amplified tapping boomed out of the wall-mounted speakers, making everyone jump. Collective disapproval wafted around like stink off a dung heap.

"Sorry," Pauley said, lips too close to her microphone. Backing off a bit, she chirped, "Better now?"

"Perfect," Jem shouted loyally. The moment was total cringe, of course. But as Pauley's only ally among the audience, she had to do her bit.

"Yay." Pauley smiled desperately down at the assembly. "Welcome. Right. Well. Happy Valentine's everyone."

Silence.

"And welcome to the 17th Annual Valentine's Day Bake Off where the Isles of Scilly's very best bakers put forth their scrummiest treats for your consideration." Gesturing around the ballroom at the crepe paper bunting and red-pink-white balloons, she added, "Absolutely spiffing set-up, wouldn't you say? Storm or no storm, we're still in business and ready to get this Bake Off started, aren't we?"

Still nothing.

Jem, whose skin had begun to crawl in sympathetic solidarity, pumped her fist and emitted a loud "Woo-hoo!" People turned and looked at her.

"Yes! That's the spirit." Pauley shot her a grateful smile. "Don't let Veronica get you down. We're all Bettys here, aren't we? No? Maybe a little too nineties with that reference."

Taking a deep breath, she segued into a canned speech about the enduring value of culinary skills and the long tradition of the Bake Off. Her voice squeaked as the words came tumbling out. Under normal circumstances, Pauley was a charming speaker. Under suboptimal—or in this case, actively hostile—conditions, she tended to go manic pixie. The *full* manic pixie.

Jem glanced around the room. The faces still looked hostile. The youngest of the stranded travelers, a brother and sister both under age ten, had fallen asleep on the carpet at their mum's feet. Or maybe they'd slipped into sugar comas. They had been fighting over drumstick squashies and ring pops—the plastic kind with a huge candy "diamond" attached. Now both kids were inert, their lips stained with blue raspberry.

At the very back of Ballroom A stood Sergeant I. Hackman, arms folded, doing his blank-faced copper routine. Jem felt sorry for him. Like the guests, Storm Veronica had also stranded him inside a posh hotel when he would be needed all over the islands, dealing with crashed boaters, elderly people without power, and who knows what else. Virtually anyone out there would be grateful for his help, so it was his rotten luck to be saddled with a bunch of toffee-nosed travelers who seemed to view their discomfort as his fault. Maybe they wanted him to take Storm Veronica into custody. From the look on his face, he expected more run-ins with the public before the storm broke.

Mercifully, Pauley's prepared remarks ended. She began introducing the bakers. Of the expected thirteen, a baker's dozen, only seven had reached St. Martin's ahead of the storm.

Up on the dais stood gangly, sad-faced Trevor Morton. A boyish forty-something with hair perpetually flopping into his face, he glared at the audience as if still bitter over the closure of his Penzance bakery. Next to him was his grandmother, Mrs. Vera Lynn Morton, smiling impartially at everyone and no one. She wore a hand-crocheted wrap over her knee-length dress. Beside Mrs. Morton was Isolde Jones, the new owner of Cake Me Proud, considered by many to have the best chance of winning. Forty-something like her ex-husband Trevor, she was sturdily built and confident looking. Her pants suit was smart, but the storm's humidity had done a number on her blonde curls. They were frizzed to the max.

She wasn't the only bad hair day. Jem and Pauley's friend Micki Latham also occupied a spot on the dais, and, like Isolde, her bountiful curls were out of control. Micki was no baker; she claimed to have trouble microwaving water. It was her cousin Clarence, an adventurous baker who never missed a chance to show off, who'd entered the contest. But when Storm Veronica blew in early, Clarence had chosen to remain with his guests at the bed & breakfast he ran, sending Micki in his place.

Beside Micki stood pink-haired Camille Carlisle. Dressed in an adorable pink maxi dress, the forty-something newcomer to St. Mary's waved at the audience. It declined to wave back. Jem hadn't been introduced to her yet. Although the island community was vanishingly small by London standards, it was still home to over two thousand people.

Rounding out the seven was the husband-and-wife duo of Keir and Posh Darden. Keir was a miniature silver fox: sixty, handsome, well-groomed, and just over five feet tall. Posh was Madonna if she'd held on to her eighties *Material Girl* persona right through to midlife; big hair, taffeta bow, and a short, ruffled skirt that belonged in an MTV museum exhibit. The pair seemed anxious. Keir bounced on his toes, while Posh looked like a slapped arse. Perhaps they feared this Bake Off would end in another humiliating loss. Staunch advocates for ultra-healthy foods, they had a tough time competing head-to-head with clotted cream and caster sugar.

Pauley was still introducing Keir and Posh when the Bake Off's judge, a local celebrity called Lemmy Beaglehole, climbed up on the dais and plucked the microphone out of Pauley's hand.

"All right, ladies and gentlemen," his voice blared from the speakers. "No more foreplay. It's time for the main event."

So that's him. Wormier looking than I expected, Jem thought.

Jem knew of Beaglehole; it was his infamously scathing viral review that had convinced her friend Micki, a wonderful vocalist, to never sing in public again. But this was the first time she'd seen the critic in the flesh.

Scrawny, apart from his incipient paunch, he had a receding hairline and neat goatee. He wouldn't have been completely unattractive if not for his painfully obvious desire for praise. Precisely how much adulation he hungered for, Jem couldn't say. But he looked as if he'd been stuck on the verge of obtaining his heart's desire for so long, his face had frozen into lines of premature triumph.

"Good afternoon, everyone. I'm Lemmy Beaglehole, your humble judge. Separating the wheat from the chaff and the sweet from the daft."

He paused for a laugh. Jem heard feet shifting under tables. Someone coughed. She would've been tempted to throw down the mic and run away, but Lemmy was probably accustomed to public face-plants. Instead of faltering, he pivoted to Pauley as if seeking to unload any discomfort on her.

"Oh, dear. Still clinging on to your fifteen minutes, are you? *Psst*, sweetheart, you're free to go. Oh, don't look so hurt. Isn't she lovely, folks? Round of applause for our own Wednesday Addams, and the last of the St. Morwenna Gwyns!"

Scant applause, mostly from Jem and Hack. Apparently seeking more of a reaction, Lemmy said, "Can you lot keep a secret? She used to be my girl."

"You—*flapdoodle!*" Whirling on him, Pauley snatched the microphone away. "First, that was a very long time ago. Second, you may be picking the winner, Lemmy, but that doesn't mean you're in charge. Go sit in the judge's seat. Now. Or I'll put you there myself."

A ripple of amusement went through the assembly. Jem heaved a sigh of relief.

Finally. They're on her side.

Pauley smiled at the assembly. Pushing a lock of magenta hair behind her ear—although a proud goth, she looked nothing like Wednesday—she continued confidently, "As I've introduced our contestants, it's time to bring out the first of their scrumptious creations. Each dessert will be presented blind, so our judge may evaluate each one for taste and visual appeal without any idea which baker it belongs to."

Pauley disappeared behind the dais's backdrop, a red curtain, taking her microphone with her. None of the contestants made eye contact with Lemmy. Rather, they stood to one side looking both hopeful and mortified, like candidates standing for public office sharing the stage with Lord Buckethead. After a couple of seconds, the red curtain rippled, and Pauley returned, pushing a trolley laden with beautifully decorated desserts.

Jem's stomach rumbled. After the judging, she would sprint for a place in the sample queue. And judging by the excited murmurs at some of the tables, she wouldn't be the only one.

"Presented for your consideration, Mr. Beaglehole, entry number one." Pauley placed the cake before him. "A double layer chocolate crumb with raspberry filling. Shaped like a heart, the universal symbol of love and romance, it's covered with dark chocolate ganache and finished with candied raspberries."

"Ah." Lemmy frowned over it. "I'm afraid someone took the name of the Valentine's Bake Off quite literally, didn't they? And, if I'm being honest, chocolate and raspberry is such an obvious combination. No points for originality." Lemmy shrugged. "All right, Pauls. Be an angel and slice me a piece. Not too large. Some of us are watching our hips."

If the barb was aimed at Pauley, she declined to receive it. Unruffled, she cut and plated a perfect wedge of cake, holding it up so everyone could admire its double layers and decadent red raspberry ooze. Jem's stomach rumbled again. If only she'd eaten a full breakfast instead of quarreling with Rhys and storming off to Pauley's house, a choice that had led to her being stranded on St. Martin's until Storm Veronica's fury abated...

"Lovely. Now on to entry number two," Pauley said, tapping a black-lacquered nail against the mic.

Startled out of her regrets, Jem sat up straight. *Pay attention. Maximum supportage*, she reminded herself. She'd braved bad weather to help Pauley, not brood over her terrible morning and uncertain future.

"This is a royal cherry trifle." Pauley held up the glass for the audience to admire. "It consists of madeira cake cut into slices, ratafia biscuits broken into pieces, cherry brandy, double cream—oh, Lord, don't we love double cream?—and cherry conserves. Plus, some whole cherries for good measure. Here you are, Lemmy."

The judge didn't respond. Why was he scowling like that? Jem thought perhaps he'd decided looking serious wasn't worrying enough to his victims.

"Lem?" Pauley nudged him.

"That first cake was a disgrace," he muttered. "Raspberry sauce must have turned." His words were close enough to the microphone to carry clearly over the speakers.

The contestants exchanged mortified glances. Although Lemmy was infamously harsh, no one had expected damning remarks right out of the gate.

With determined brightness, Pauley said, "All right, Lemmy, this is still just the tasting phase. So, let's move on to entry number two." She spooned out a generous portion of the trifle. To Jem's un-judgy eyes, it looked magnificent.

"But that bloody sauce wrecked my palate," Lemmy complained, voice cracking. "My throat's on fire. I need water. Get me water."

Pauley looked around helplessly. A few guests were drinking bottled water, but no one seemed to have an unopened one to share. Beside her, Lemmy shuddered, pushing the trifle away. "How can I eat that? Looks like something the dog sicked up."

"Just taste it, why don't you," called someone in the audience.

"Because my tongue's gone numb." Lemmy looked around wildly. "Water! Where is it?"

Someone in the front row relented, passing up a bottle of water. Hands shaking, Lemmy clumsily twisted off the lid. He knocked back a great quantity—or tried to. The water came spewing back out like the squirt of a spiteful dolphin.

"Lemmy!" Pauley cried.

The judge tried to answer, but no sounds came. His face was dead white; cords stood out on his neck. In a struggle to rise, he kicked over his chair. Tottering around the table, Lemmy made it halfway to the stairs before a massive spasm shook his entire body. The water bottle fell from his hands. Then he toppled off the stage.

"Poison," someone cried. "Help him, he's been poisoned!"

Jem ran to his side but could do nothing. Hack tried to render aid, but Lemmy's thrashing limbs kept him at bay. Micki, who'd seized the microphone, was asking the stranded holidaymakers if there was a doctor in the house. Meanwhile, one of the panicked guests kept insisting that someone ring 999, which she'd apparently forgotten was impossible. Even if the Bay View's manager could have hailed St. Mary's by shortwave radio, no rescue helicopter or coastguard vessel would reach St. Martin's until conditions improved. To do otherwise meant almost certain injury or death for the would-be rescuers.

He's on his own. We all are, Jem thought, watching Lemmy's movements weaken.

In five minutes, it was over. The most hated critic in Cornwall was a corpse.

And if whoever poisoned that cake is in the Bay View, we'll be trapped overnight with a murderer.

2

THE STORM BEFORE THE STORM

"Because you're an idiot!" Jemima Jago shrieked at the man she loved, and meant it.

"*I'm* the idiot?" Rhys glared at her. "After working my fingers to the bone for the last few days because *you* asked me to?"

"I asked you to tidy up. Two words. Tidy. Up."

Jem turned away from the window, where the early morning sun chose this inauspicious moment to poke its head out from behind a cloud. If it had any decency, it would go back down and come up again, because its first attempt had been a total disaster.

Operating on pure fury, she yanked open a drawer, grabbing an indiscriminate fistful of knickers. She wasn't sure what she was choosing, but it hardly mattered. Her suitcase was still packed. Less than ten minutes ago, she'd strolled into Tremayne Cottage, the home she shared with Rhys, towing the wheeled luggage that had sustained her during her job-seeking trip to the mainland. Now all she had to do was grab the handle, turn around, and tow it back out the door.

"But I spent hours tidying up." Rhys followed her into the bedroom. He had to climb over his weight bench to do it, an action he seemed to find entirely natural. "Just because it's not one hundred percent perfect—"

"Perfect? Rhys! You told me I'd be amazed."

"I thought you would be. I fell behind. So sue me."

"You said you finished painting the living room."

"I was projecting ahead. It *would* have been all painted, but you turned up early."

"Two hours early. Do you mean to say you think it only lacks two hours' work?"

He threw up his hands as if she were the unreasonable one.

"And our bedroom," Jem said, gesturing at the heaps and piles obscuring most of the floor and furniture. "You've turned it into mini storage."

"Temporarily. And only because I thought tidying the living room was top priority. God knows you're always banging on about it."

"You know why? Because it's unbearable. If you were going to the trouble of shifting your exercise junk, why didn't you stow it in the lighthouse? Like I asked," she huffed. "Instead, you jammed it all in here. And why didn't you pack up this dog training grot? Instead of dumping it all on our bed."

"It's not grot." Rhys's chin jutted stubbornly. "Just because Buck washed out of the Doggone Olympics last year doesn't mean he won't win a ribbon next year. *I'm* not giving up on him."

The accusation in his voice made Jem want to scream. Before she could, the aforementioned Buck, a small, spotted white dog of ambiguous heritage, barked uneasily from his vantage point under the weight bench. Inability to perform complex maneuvers under bright lights notwithstanding, he was a clever little guy. He knew this row between his beloved Rhys and his adored Jem had escalated far beyond the usual, and like any small person caught in the crossfire, he wanted to take the temperature down a notch.

Jem sighed. She was furious, but of course it had nothing to do with Buck. If anything, it had to do with Valentine's Day, a completely wretched, fake, made-up-by-greeting-card-sellers holiday that pumped up singletons with false hope and then popped them by knifepoint.

She'd wanted to spend all of Valentine's Day with Rhys, and because Storm Veronica was moving toward Cornwall much faster than originally predicted, Jem had risen before dawn, hurrying back to St. Morwenna on her little boat, *Bellatrix*. Based on extensive texting with Rhys, she'd arrived at Tremayne Cottage expecting a completely redone living room. More fool her.

Instead, she'd found a living room with the furniture gone, one wall painted, drop cloths and paint cans every-where, and a deep groove in the middle of the floor. Rhys claimed not to know when it had appeared or what had caused it, but it didn't take an amateur detective to guess that a loaded barbell had been dropped. Which was why anyone but the laziest person would have unloaded the weights and moved them in stages, not tried powerlifting on parade.

Next, Jem had retreated to the bedroom, where she'd found all Rhys's weight training gadgets shoehorned in with their bedroom furniture. As for the bed, it was covered in chew toys, dog stuffies, plastic rings, Buck's fleece bed, and his smelly, hair-covered blanket.

"Don't fret, mate. It's not your fault," Rhys told the dog.

The unspoken implication—*We know whose fault it really is*—made Jem's blood boil.

"That's right, Buck, you're completely innocent," she said, looking into the dog's bright button eyes. He blinked unhappily. If ever a dog's face pleaded, *Don't bring me into this*, Buck's did, but she was too angry to choose mercy.

"It's not your fault he only keeps his promises to you," Jem informed the dog. "If you're due for the vet, he gets you there. If you need extra practice for the Doggone Olympics, he remakes the living room into your training course. But if I want something, it looks like I have to do it myself."

"Then why don't you, now that you're back. I have a commissioned painting to finish." Rhys sounded cold. "Also two boats in need of a repaint. Both paying jobs. One of us needs to earn a living."

Jem stopped dead, staring at him. Last November, a clash with her former boss at Penzance's venerable Courtney Library had led to Jem impulsively offering her resignation. At the time, she'd been neck-deep in a murder case—only a day away from solving it and saving a young boy's life in the process—and the attitude of Mr. Lancelot Atherton, her supervisor, had been as smugly patriarchal as his name.

While the publicity for her first case had been touch-and-go (she'd been arrested) and on her third case had been delicate (she'd made an enemy of Detective Sergeant Conrad, the eight-hundred-pound gorilla of the Exeter murder squad), both the media and the public seemed charmed by Jem's second career as the Scilly Sleuth. When Mr. Atherton said he'd have to sack her if she didn't give it up, she'd responded by resigning—or, if she was being honest, threatening to resign. She'd expected Mr. Atherton to back off. Instead, he'd said yes. Enthusiastically.

So, yes, she'd mucked it up. Mr. Atherton had pushed her into choosing between the profession she loved and solving a mystery with a ticking clock. She'd done the latter, basked in the adoration, patted herself on the back for saving a life... and woke up a few days later to find herself jobless for the first time since freshman year.

Still. The unfairness of Rhys's attitude stung. It wasn't as if she'd spent weeks and weeks painting her toenails and watching telly. Except for Christmas week and New Year's, she'd spent every day reading job listings, calling old friends from the library world, and dropping in on private libraries and universities to get a feel for their staffing needs. Everyone she talked to was encouraging. They assured her the solution was simple. Just move back to London.

In London, she could find a job long before she could score a flat, and her work life would resume with barely a hiccup. Yes, she'd have to give up Rhys, and Pauley, and Micki, and Kenzie, and Clarence, not to mention the entire community of St. Morwenna, plus the Isles of Scilly themselves and the ever-beautiful, often terrifying Celtic Sea. But that was the best—and perhaps only—way for her to resume her career. Amateur sleuthing was, after all, an unpaid gig.

"Don't look at me like that." Rhys folded his arms across his chest. "You've been out of work for months. Volunteering at the Hugh Town Library brings in nothing. And making trips to the mainland every week costs petrol."

"I make those trips to do little jobs. While I keep trying to land a big job."

She'd managed to bring in a tiny amount by taking on short-term consulting jobs for historical societies, but the societies paid their own officers little or nothing, so that sort of work was akin to a donation. Lately she'd even started brainstorming ways to reinvent herself as Jem Jago, Special Collections Librarian for Hire. Maybe in another era it would have worked. But now, in the age of austerity, not to mention anti-intellectualism, libraries struck many people as relics from a bygone age. Pauley had suggested she write a book—a sort of thinly-disguised autobiography about a librarian sleuth—but Jem wasn't sure. She'd always done things in her own way, according to her own rhythms. Deadlines made her queasy.

"And I spoke to the Chough Society chair yesterday," she added. "They'll hire me in early March to catalog their library."

"Yeah, but that's temporary. And is it even paid?"

She looked away.

"Because Bettie Quick's offer still stands," Rhys went on. "She'll hire you to run the Ice Cream Hut for the entire season, spring and summer, starting the first of April. That would bring in enough to keep us going. Unless you still think working an island job is beneath you."

"You bastard." She shook her head. "You absolute bastard. It's not about what's beneath me. I trained to be a librarian. Of course, I want to work in my chosen field."

"Then why'd you quit? Why didn't you say 'Yes, sir' to Atherton, work on the murder case anyway, and dare the little weasel to try and sack you? He couldn't have managed it without months or years of mediation. You could've held on to the job with nothing worse than a dent in your pride. But you always have to prove how independent you are. Just like—" He broke off.

"Don't stop." For a moment when Rhys was enumerating Bettie Quick's generous offer, Jem's eyes had prickled, warning of imminent tears. Now she felt nothing but stone-cold rage. "Just like what? Just like when I talked Cam into going out with us on the boat?"

He groaned.

"What? If you want us to go back to that, fine. Let's go back to it." Jem's voice was steady, but inside she was cold with fear as well as fury. He no longer blamed her for the accident that took his little brother's life. Why was she bringing it up again now?

Rhys took a deep breath. Raking both hands through his hair, he pressed his lips together, seeming to swallow whatever he meant to say.

Jem's pulse thudded in her throat as she waited. Every time she thought this particular ghost was exorcised, it rematerialized, rattling floorboards and snuffing candles.

Finally, Rhys said, "How about you don't put words in my mouth. I only meant, when you want to go your own way, you do it." He knelt to pet Buck, clearly focusing on the dog's response instead of hers. "You've been going your own way with the job thing for weeks. I've tried to man up about it. But I'm working more than ever and you're finding fault with everything."

"The place is a wreck. You admitted that before you moved in. You promised me you'd clean up. I could have—"

"You would've used that as an excuse to bin everything!"

"No, but even if I did, wouldn't that be better than this? A wrecked living room? A bedroom we can't even breathe in?"

Rhys continued to play with Buck, gently pulling the dog's ears.

"Could you look at me?"

"I think I'm done talking."

"Fine." Jem looked around for the tote bag she'd meant

to fill and couldn't find it. All she had was that handful of knickers. And her suitcase beside the door, still packed up and ready to go.

When she climbed the weight bench blocking the door, Buck whined and Rhys jerked back.

"Hey! That's my face you almost kicked!"

"Won't happen again." Jem marched through the living room, resisting the urge to kick a half-empty bucket of paint on the way. There was a cobweb up in one corner, which Rhys had declined to pull down while painting the wall six inches away. If he hadn't been an artist, she would've told him to get his eyes tested.

"Where are you going?"

"Not your problem."

"So that's it? You're leaving me?"

"Well-spotted!" She slammed the door in her wake.

~

Outside Tremayne Cottage, Storm Veronica hung over the northwest like a clump of grievances, swollen with unshed tears. A cold wind swept in off the sea. The kind of weather that foretells the end of something.

Maybe it will fizzle. Or veer off to Ireland.

Jem set out, grass squelching under her trainers. Another gust tossed her waist-length hair, which she'd let down on the way to the cottage and forgotten to pin back up. Unbidden, she imagined herself as the heroine from a paperback Gothic from the 1960s in which a woman, usually in a white nightgown, fled from a lonely mansion, eyes wide, long hair flying. Except for the time—early morning instead of midnight—and the props—wheeled luggage instead of a lantern—it was a perfect fit.

Proof I'm a librarian first, Jem thought. *I can't even walk out on my boyfriend without seeing myself on the cover of a Dorothy Daniels novel.*

Usually, when she made a big decision, the second-guessing set in immediately. This time, her internal Greek chorus was silent. Maybe that meant leaving Rhys was the right thing to do.

When she arrived at the Byway, a long, paved road that bisected St. Morwenna, the wind gusted harder, slamming her with such force, it felt like a shove toward her destination: Lyonesse House, the home of her best friend, Pauley Gwyn.

Jem shivered. Not only had she forgotten to deal with her hair, she'd left her mac on the peg in Rhys's foyer. Fortunately, her old room at Lyonesse House still contained plenty of her essentials, including at least one coat.

One coat? Half my wardrobe is still there. Half my books, too.

Jem had procrastinated endlessly about finishing her move to Tremayne Cottage, leaning on everything from the weather to the holidays to explain why she'd left so much stored at Pauley's. Now her true motive came clear.

I knew how he is. I knew how I am. And I knew I'd be back at Lyonesse House, sooner rather than later.

Jem had the Byway, which in summer would have been thick with locals and tourists, all to herself. But she wasn't totally alone; on her left and right, yellow-slickered figures dotted the fields of Hobson's Farm. They were harvesting narcissi, the Isles of Scilly's principal export. Even without the threat of Storm Veronica, the crop had to be brought in early. Weeks before Easter, the narcissi would be shipped out, to be sold in florists' shops all over England.

Just as Lyonesse House came into view, the heavens

opened and the rain beat down, the drops fat and cold. Picking up her suitcase and awkwardly clutching it to her chest, Jem sprinted the last thousand yards. The oldest home in the Isles of Scilly, built in the seventeenth century and renovated many times since, Lyonesse House squatted behind crumbling hedgerows and a broken gate. It reminded Jem of a cranky old bull, snoozing in the pasture.

She ignored the front door, which was now kept locked twenty-four hours a day and seven days a week, the consequence of a near-fatal break-in. Instead, Jem made for the back door, which opened onto the kitchen. Just as she reached the threshold it swung open to reveal Pauley Gwyn, hands on hips. She was already in full goth plumage, with blood-red nails and a black lace apron.

"There you are! With luggage, I see. And looking like a windblown witch," she added, shutting the door and bolting it against the wind, which rattled it hard. "What's up? Going door to door flogging ladies' underthings?"

"What?"

"In your hand. Knickers. Not even sexy. Cotton."

Pauley was right. Jem had left Rhys gripping her suitcase handle with one hand and a bunch of knickers with the other. Thank goodness none of those flower pickers had paused in their work to say hello, or she would have looked quite mad.

"Can I assume the choice of knickers means you've returned for good? Resuming a celibate life?"

"Rhys rang, didn't he?"

Pauley ignored that. "You didn't even ask how I managed to open the door at exactly the right moment."

"Oh. Erm... psychic?"

"I've been peeking out the window for you. The

weather report says the storm may miss us, but either way, the sea will still be choppy. Best to start out extra early."

"Start early for what?"

Pauley waved her spatula in a threatening manner. "Think."

Jem was at a total loss. Then she remembered her original plan. Rise before dawn, sail from the mainland to St. Morwenna, admire Rhys's handiwork, retire to the bedroom for a leisurely Valentine's reunion—they *had* been separated for six days, after all—and then help out Pauley, who was Mistress of Ceremonies at the Annual Valentine's Day Bake Off on St. Martin's.

Jem groaned. "Oh, Pauls, I don't know..."

"If you've gone off Rhys, you have nothing to do but be my assistant for the day," Pauley said, spatula shaking menacingly. "Plenty of sweets on St. Martin's to keep your mind off him. And who knows, maybe you'll get lucky."

"Lucky how?"

"Maybe someone will get murdered."

3

"IT'LL LOOK EXTRA ROMANTIC WHEN IT'S SWEPT OUT TO SEA"

Jem sniffed the air. "What's that you're baking? I thought you weren't participating."

"Just because I'm not entering the competition doesn't mean I'm not bringing treats. You're smelling two things. My famous cappuccino cake, which is still in the oven, and my breakfast tarts. Have one."

Jem accepted a plate containing three golden-brown pastries, still warm. The first bite made her groan with pleasure.

"It's divine. What's in it?"

"Ham, ricotta, and leeks. Good lord, watching you eat is like *Shark Week*. At least sit down. I'll put the kettle on."

Jem did as she was bid. Between tart number two and tart number three, she announced, "I've left Rhys."

Pauley removed the cake from the oven and left it to cool on the rack. As she veered toward the electric kettle, it began to *ding*. Pouring the hot water into two stoneware mugs, she said, "I hope you don't mind drinking up my left-over Christmas blend. I'm on another savings kick. Using up every single thing in my cupboard before I do another mainland shop."

"Did you hear what I said? I left Rhys. It's over." Jem wiped her mouth and dusted crumbs from her lap. "That means I'm staying with you again, at least for the time being. Hope that's okay."

"Fine. I'll play along," Pauley said. "What did you row about this time? No, let me guess. You say he's a ruddy slob and passive-aggressive as all get out. He says you can't find library work and won't take an island job. Am I right? Should I pack up my crystal ball and my tambourine and take my psychic show on the road?"

"I'm out looking for work every single week," Jem retorted, stung all over again. "The only jobs available in the Scillies are for teenagers or pensioners. And he *is* passive-aggressive. He told me he'd clean the cottage while I was gone, and instead he made everything a hundred times worse. And expected me to thank him for it!"

She overemphasized that last bit because her argument clearly wasn't doing it. The silence stretched out uncomfortably.

"Anyway," Jem said at last. "If it's done steeping, I really would like some tea."

"I ought to pour it over your head." Pauley thumped Jem's mug down in front of her, splashing a little, and took the opposite chair. "Didn't I tell you not to move in with him? The cottage wasn't ready. Didn't I say, take it slow? Live here and see Rhys on date nights. And didn't I say that if you didn't find work soon, he'd start eating his heart out over money? He's been on his own forever, Jemmie. He works three jobs. He has nightmares about losing everything and winding up on the dole."

"Is that all you have for me? I told you so?"

"No. I did mention you look like a witch."

"So do you. Daily."

"Yes, but by choice. You're lucky I kept your old room ready. And you're welcome to stay as long as you like. But." She stabbed a finger at Jem. "Now that I've fed you, I expect repayment. Freshen up and dress in layers. You know how cold St. Martin's can be at this time of year."

"Come on, Pauls. Have you looked outside? If we go, and the sea gets too choppy, we might get stranded."

"Nobody's getting stranded. The storm will miss us. Last night the news gave it only a twenty percent chance of hitting the Scillies."

"This morning my app said fifty."

"They don't know," Pauley said breezily. "Forecasters, apps, it doesn't matter. This is my first year as Mistress of Ceremonies and I'm not about to no-show because I'm scared of a little rain."

"Fine, go. But don't make me tag along." The words came out rather whiny, making Jem cringe. But the truth was, she would have liked nothing better than to stay home alone, especially if it stormed. Ensconcing herself in one of Lyonesse House's window seats with a book on her lap, staring out a rain-streaked pane toward a bleak brown landscape, suited her mood precisely. "I mean, I'll help you gather the decorations and pack up..."

"Oh, I see. Staying alone ten minutes away from Tremayne Cottage is your plan. You want to moon around this old heap, hoping and praying that Rhys slinks over to say sorry..."

Jem bristled. "Certainly not. And he wouldn't."

"He would. I guarantee it. And he'd expect to find you here, pretending to read a book, ready to kiss and make up."

"Fine. I'll go with you to St. Martin's. But if the waves get too big, the ferries won't fetch us back."

"Then we'll each bring an overnight bag. It's a posh hotel. Can't think of a better place to be stranded."

A narrow strip of beach curled around the western tip of the island of St. Martin's. An exuberant white brush stroke, it separated jagged granite rocks from the viridian sea. Overlooking that beach sat the Bay View Hotel, the most luxurious destination in the Isles of Scilly not located on Tresco. Built only ten years ago, the Bay View ably impersonated a storied old heap. If Jem hadn't known any better, she would've assumed it was a property that had been passed down through the generations, from piracy to respectability, until a great-grandchild sold it to escape the tax bill. The Bay View exuded hedonism but not vulgarity; it was a holiday spot for the best sort of people, who could indulge without making a spectacle of themselves.

"Doesn't it look romantic with all those brooding clouds on the horizon?" Pauley asked Jem.

"Yeah. It'll look extra romantic when it's swept out to sea," said Bart the Ferryman, who didn't let a small task like tying his boat up by the water stairs interrupt a steady stream of complaints. He'd spent the entire trip grumbling about everything. The sea spray, the rough waves, the February weather in general, and the Bay View's management in particular.

"Poncy gits and their photo ID," he muttered. Around his neck hung a lanyard bearing the hated identification required in order for him to pick up and drop off guests at the Bay View's private dock. The portrait was dark and blurry, like a Bigfoot picture. Bart wasn't a fan of furnishing references, and he was allergic to official photographs. Jem had a number of theories as to why, but he had yet to kill anyone, so there was that. Moreover, his service—such as it was—remained the cheapest around the Isles of Scilly, and as it had been recently pointed out, she was unemployed. "But if you want to drown with them, that's your lookout."

"We can't be the only people you've ferried to St. Martin's?"

"I took a few donuts, first thing. A lady with pink hair. Oh, and a pair of tossers who never stopped bickering," Bart said. "Everyone else canceled. You're the only pair mad enough to set out this late."

"Late? It's only half-nine. And the storm will miss us. Those clouds will blow away, you'll see," Pauley said.

Jem glanced at the sky. It looked worse than ever. She wore a light jacket over her cable knit sweater and jeans but had once again forgotten her mac. The waves already seemed bigger than was safe for Bart's ferry, and over the sea Storm Veronica loomed blacker than ever. Would the baking contestants really risk this? The food fair vendors? The audience?

As they disembarked, Pauley asked, "Well, what do you think of the Bay View? Pretty grand, eh?" She'd put herself in charge of the Bake Off decorations; Jem had custody of the cappuccino cake. Pauley had packed the precious cargo in an old Christmas tin in case Jem dropped it, which she was wont to do.

"Amazing. Can't possibly be so posh on the inside."

"Nope. It's better." Pauley elbowed her conspiratorially. "Surprise! We're booked for the night."

In spite of herself, Jem squealed. Pauley squealed back —they'd always been contagious squealers—and they were jumping up and down in glee when Bart trudged down the gangplank, dropping Pauley's box at her feet.

"Whew." He wiped his forehead theatrically. "I reckon that calls for a tip, milady."

"Sure. Here's my top tip. Don't call women 'milady.'" Pauley hefted the box, which contained only paper banners, uninflated balloons, and other featherweight items. "Unless you're planning to kidnap said women, in which case it's fine. Expected, really."

"Pair of harpies, the both of you." Bart tromped back up the way he'd come, re-boarding *Merry Maid*. "Don't expect me to risk my neck ferrying you back to St. Morwenna. The storm will be a direct hit. I can feel it. I'm going to find a safe berth and hole up."

"Oh, come on, Bart. Don't forget who got rid of your biggest competitor," Jem called cheerfully, referring to her last case.

He pulled up the gangplank. "What have you done for me lately, Scilly Sleuth?"

"Paid you!" Pauley said tartly. "And you'd better not leave us stranded for revenge or I'll report you to the council. See if I don't," she added, though without real heat. To Jem's knowledge, Bart had never stranded anyone overnight. And no trip aboard his ferry was complete without him attempting to wheedle more money out of a passenger, or that passenger shouting imprecations at *Merry Maid* as she putted away.

As Jem turned back to the hotel, lightning flashed overhead. Two seconds later it was followed by a long, resounding boom.

"He's right. The storm is close," Jem said. "All we can hope is that it passes quickly. Do you really think the bakers and audience will show?"

"Well, it looks like there are plenty of people milling around on the porch," Pauley said. "Besides, we're here now, so the die is cast. Care to go inside and see what extravagance awaits?"

"Yes, please."

"That's the spirit." Pauley shifted the box, balancing it against her hip. "This isn't heavy, but it *is* bulky. Run ahead and open that door for me, will you?"

The path led Jem past deserted beach tables and closed umbrellas. While she found the weather pleasantly brisk, most holidaymakers would probably call it cold. As for those people milling about on the porch, they looked too miserable to be Bake Off enthusiasts or vendor hall shoppers. Bundled up in coats, hats, and gloves, most sat on or leaned against pieces of luggage. Some fiddled with their mobiles, trying to find coverage. Others shielded their eyes and stared at the bay, perhaps willing another ferry to appear where *Merry Maid* had so briefly docked.

Probably waiting on charters, Jem thought. But the fact Bart had declined to ask if anyone would prefer to take a chance on his beat-up old ferry was a very bad sign. Bart loved nothing more than poaching customers. To give up the chance meant his sailor's instincts predicted very dire conditions indeed.

Well, if their charters are delayed, they can always attend the Bake Off. Unless the storm makes it a total dud.

For Pauley's sake, she hoped not. Surely some of the vendors would make it, selling the usual mix of island goodies: homemade chutney, beaded jewelry, knitted scarfs, postcards, calendars, and Scillonian wine. Or if they'd had enough local color, they could always take advantage of the Bay View's cozy-looking wine bar, which Jem had read about while perusing the resort's website. There was also a boutique library she was eager to check out. Februarys were made for hot toddies, overstuffed armchairs, and books.

Making it through the crowd to the foyer's outer door, Jem held it open, allowing Pauley to scoot into the gloomy space. She shifted her big box of party favors again.

"Sure you can handle that?"

"Yes, it's just unwieldy. Open the inner door."

Watching her friend over her shoulder, Jem pushed open the foyer's inner door. Stepping backward into the Bay View's lobby, she released the door, turned, and tripped over a body.

4

A PROTEST, A POLICEMAN, AND A PREMONITION

Falling, Jem yelped. Pinwheeling her arms and trying impossibly to regain her balance, impressions tumbled through her mind—the leg she'd tripped over, delicate porcelain vases, soaring floral arrangements, navy-blue carpet. She expected to face-plant on the corpse, which would be a new low, even for her. Instead, a pair of big, strong hands caught her from behind.

"Isn't this how we met, Stargazer?"

She recognized the voice instantly. It belonged to Sergeant I. Hackman, also known as Hack, the Isles of Scilly's top cop. But before she could answer him, the body on the floor moved. Its bony hand seized her ankle in a cold grip. Jem shrieked.

"Sorry, love. But you've already bruised my leg. Couldn't let you step on my face."

The speaker, not actually dead despite her posture, was a stringy old woman, north of seventy-five but probably south of a hundred. Her lemon-yellow dress was long enough to preserve modesty but short enough to reveal a pair of knobbly knees. Pale eyes twinkled from behind wire-framed specs; her steel-gray curls, unnaturally thick and plentiful, might have been a wig.

"What are you doing on the floor?" Jem screamed.

"No need to shout. As for why I'm down here, that's what we were discussing when you stumbled in." She looked past Jem. "Hiya, Pauley."

"Hiya, Mrs. Jones. Need a hand up?"

"Certainly not. I'm staging a protest, love," said Mrs. Jones calmly. "It's called passive resistance. I've stationed myself here, at the very threshold of an unfair and illegitimate contest, to bring awareness to my cause. Effect positive change."

"Excuse me? Unfair? Illegitimate?" Pauley put down her box, the better to glare at the old woman. "You'd better not be referring to the Bake Off. The committee and I spent a lot of time preparing for it, and I won't listen to anyone who insults our—"

"Please, let's not relitigate all that," Hack broke in. "I assure you, I've heard the full and comprehensive list of Mrs. Jones's concerns. I have no opinion on the Bake Off's merits either way. There's only one issue for me. Obstructing the entrance and/or egress of a business is unlawful. Legal protests are to be held out-of-doors, in an orderly fashion. Also with the proper permits, in the case of St. Martin's. Mrs. Jones, as long as you persist in this, you're risking health and safety."

"Nonsense, my health is fine. It doesn't hurt me to lie down for a while."

"Ms. Jago almost took a header into the carpet."

"Clumsy," the old woman sniffed. "Not my problem."

"But it *is* your problem," Hack said with the sort of determined pleasantness that signaled he was on the verge of losing his temper. Jem had some familiarity with the process. Until today, they'd gone weeks without speaking. The previous autumn, they'd suffered a blow-up over her theory of a certain murder case. In the end, she'd been left smarting over his contemptuous attitude. And he'd been left with egg on his face when she was publicly proven right.

"I told you," Hack reminded Mrs. Jones, "guests have a right to clear walkways, free of impediments."

"Once my demands are met, they'll get it."

"Mrs. Jones." Hack forced a smile. "Storm Veronica is almost upon us. I expect it to keep me busy. I need to get back to the station so I can do my job. Do you think it's fair that you made the hotel manager divert me to St. Martin's? And for such a silly situation?"

"But if you'd only play along, we could wrap this up in nothing flat," Mrs. Jones said. "It's easy to ignore a little old lady on the floor. But a big, handsome man in uniform, looming over me with such menace? No one could turn away from that spectacle." She nodded at Hack's duty belt. "Cuff me. Attach me to that credenza. People will be outraged, and Pauley will be forced to appease me."

"I don't even know what you want," Pauley cried.

"I'm not going to cuff you," Hack said. "But if you don't get up under your own steam, I'll pick you up and carry you out to my boat. You can go with me to the station and be photographed and fingerprinted and DNA swabbed."

"Oh, fine, then, don't. Just lend me the cuffs and I'll attach myself to the credenza. You don't have to admit to being my accomplice," she added. "You can say I took them away from you."

A flash of movement in the reception area caught Jem's eye. Though the check-in desk was unattended, a faint rustling made her turn. She saw no one. Just a tall potted plant, leaves rippling slightly.

Did the staff run away rather than watch this? Jem wondered.

Another flicker of motion drew her gaze toward one of the reception area's wide ornamental columns. A man peeped out from around the corner, eyes raking the scene until they met Jem's. Then he disappeared behind the barrier again.

Pauley said, "Mrs. Jones, I can't believe you're willing to get arrested over this, and risk spending the storm in the clink. It sounds like I'm the person you need to talk to. Why don't we go to the café and order a pot of tea? Then you can explain—"

"I won't be bought off with builder's," the old woman snapped. "Lemmy Beaglehole is a disgrace. The very idea that a person of his low character, a notorious poison pen, would be permitted to judge this competition—well, it proves the fix is in. As Mistress of Ceremonies, I call upon you to meet the demands of the B.A.B."

"What's that?" Jem asked.

"Bakers Against Beaglehole."

"And what are your demands?" Pauley asked.

"Immediate repudiation and removal of one Lemuel Dardington Beaglehole, known more infamously as—"

"Gran!"

The foyer's inner door flew open with such force, Jem, Pauley, and Hack scattered to avoid being hit. In marched a short, sturdy, forty-something woman. Over her trackies she wore a mens' mac that fell to her knees. In ordinary circumstances, the woman might have been pleasant to look at, given her large brown eyes, heart-shaped face, and shoulder-length blonde curls. But her hair was frizzy, courtesy of Storm Veronica, and a deep crimson blotch covered her throat. She looked like a woman on the verge. Maybe of a crying jag. Maybe of criminal assault.

"Gran. I want you... up off... that floor... this instant..." Between gasps, she pressed a hand to her chest. "Lord. When the manager... told me... I ran... all the way."

"And you seem to have survived." Mrs. Jones's eyes sparkled. "But, Isolde, you really ought to take a Zumba class. The shop's only a half mile away."

Isolde groaned. Or maybe she growled. Jem thought the noise sounded like Miss Piggy being put through the wringer.

"Gran! I'm not out of shape. The winds are practically gale force. I fell down twice."

"I see you're wearing Trevor's mac again." Mrs. Jones tutted. "You really must stop using his things whenever it suits you. Don't you think poor Trev might need his mac on a day like this?"

That seemed to hit Isolde where she stood. Mouth twisting, she said, "Gran, I can't mess about with you all morning. I have to box up my cake and get ready to appear on stage. Even if there's no audience and I'm one of three contestants, I intend to properly represent Cake Me Proud. Unless you force Sergeant Hackman to arrest you, in which case I'll die of shame."

"Nonsense. I'm taking radical action on behalf of the B.A.B. When my demands are met, all the contestants will benefit."

"I can assure you, no matter what you say or do, Lemmy is judging this Bake Off," Pauley said implacably. "He's under contract. End of story."

From her supine position, Mrs. Jones appeared to consider her next move. Looking toward the foyer, Jem realized that many of the bundled-up, luggage-bearing folks from the porch stood close to the glass, peering inside and hoping to enter. Given Isolde's description of the winds, it made sense.

"Suppose he doesn't show," Mrs. Jones asked Pauley hopefully. "Will you judge the event yourself?"

"He's already here. Arrived at eight o'clock and texted me twice to complain about the eggs Benedict."

"I assure you, there's nothing wrong with the Bay View's eggs Benedict," said a voice from behind the wide ornamental column.

"Mr. Fernsby," Hack snapped, whirling. "So glad you've turned up. I'm afraid I have no choice but to arrest Mrs. Jones. Since you manage this hotel and flagged me down to request her removal, could you come out and witness this, please? Just to ensure the process is smooth and professional?"

Fernsby, a doughy man with a bright red tie and big round specs to match his big round face, emerged from his hiding place. At the same time, the potted plant rustled again, and a wide-eyed young woman in an Ann Taylor trouser suit crept out as well.

"Why did you flag down a copper when you'd already called me?" Isolde demanded.

Fernsby winced. He looked like every hotel manager Jem had ever met, which was admittedly only a handful: tie askew, brow furrowed, visibly weighed down by the sheer breadth of his duties. He might have been thirty or sixty; his eyes had the hollowness of a customer service veteran.

"We tried to call you first," offered the young woman, apparently the Bay View's check-in clerk. Her brown hair was pulled back in a messy ponytail; the shoulder pads on her vintage suit made her look like a child playing dress-up. "You didn't answer, and he saw Sergeant Hackman tie up at the dock. It was only after he started talking to Mrs. Jones that you picked up."

"I was baking in the shop. You must've rung my home line next door." Isolde looked from Fernsby to his assistant. "I mean, really. Could you two be less professional, hiding like that?"

"I wasn't hiding. I was observing in an unobtrusive manner," Fernsby said.

"I was scared," the young woman volunteered. "I thought my premonition was coming true."

Mrs. Jones sat up. "What premonition?" She seemed to take that far more seriously than Hack's threat of arrest.

"I dreamed about a woman dead on the floor." The desk clerk hugged herself nervously. "It was terrifying. It seemed so real. When I saw you lying there, I thought you'd... you know. Passed on."

"Don't be ridiculous. I'll bury the lot of you," Mrs. Jones said. "You! The one who bruised my leg. Help me up."

The moment the way was clear, the dam at the entrance broke, and several luggage-bearing guests flooded in. So did a person carrying a cake box, though they melted into the press off bodies too quickly for Jem to note his or her particulars. Still, it was a good sign—at least one more entry for the contest.

Smoothing her dress and picking up her bag from where she'd left it on the floor, Mrs. Jones gave Isolde an impish smile. "There now. Crisis averted. Go home, box up that cake, and put on something nice. This will be your big triumph, I'm sure of it."

Looking as if she'd like to deliver one of Miss Piggy's signature karate chops, Isolde said with injured dignity, "Yes. Well. If you're *quite* finished creating turmoil, I reckon I'll head back. When I dashed out, I may have left the doors to the shop unlocked again. Someone could be rifling the till, stealing me blind."

"Don't fret, love. St. Martin's is as safe as it ever was," Mrs. Jones said breezily. "I've lived here my whole life, I ought to know." She turned to Jem. "Don't I know you?"

"Maybe. I'm Jem Jago. You know, the Scilly Sleuth."

"Of course. I should have recognized you. My friend Mrs. Morton and I have positively been on tenterhooks waiting for the next crime. But if it can't be a murder, a bake off is the next best thing." To Pauley, she added, "If you're still offering that pot of tea, I accept. We've another three and a half hours until the contest. Plenty of time for me to convince you to sack Beaglehole and step into the breach."

"I've told you, Lemmy's under contract. My hands are tied," Pauley said, hefting her decorations. "What's more, I need to put the finishing touches on Ballroom A. *And* scope out our room." She grinned at Jem. "I checked in online last night, so that's all settled. I'll pick up our keys and go have a look."

"I hope it has a good view of the sea," Jem said. "The wave action should be spectacular."

"It's a garden view. But gratis," Pauley reminded her. "Look at all these poor souls hoping to get home. At least we're settled for the duration. I'll text you when I'm done setting up." As she started toward the lifts, she said over her shoulder, "Bye, Mrs. Jones. Cheers, Hack."

"Cheers." Hack turned to Jem. "See you around, Stargazer. I'm off to launch the RIB while there's still time to get back to St. Mary's."

"RIB?" said one of the thwarted travelers who'd just come in from the porch. "You mean, rigid inflatable? It was swept out to sea, mate."

Hack stared at him. "But it was tied up."

"Oh, it's still on the line. Just upside down and rolling with the waves. Whatever you had stowed on the deck is fish food."

Swearing, Hack dashed out headlong into the wind. Jem watched him run down the flagstone path and disappear from sight.

"Oh, dear," Mrs. Jones murmured serenely. If she blamed herself for Hack's predicament, she gave no sign. Hooking her arm through Jem's, she maneuvered them to face away from the check-in desk, deeper inside the hotel.

"See that lounge on the other side of the common room? It's a wine bar. Very posh, but they'll make us a pot of tea. You did say you're buying?"

"Of course," Jem muttered. Maybe she could charge it to their gratis room?

"Now. I find that policeman completely snoggable, don't you agree? I do enjoy a man in uniform." Still clutching Jem's arm, the old woman forged ahead, pulling Jem in her wake. "Bit too young for my taste, if I'm being honest. Besides, I suspect he rather fancies you. You can tell me if you fancy him back over a nice cuppa. And since you're fond of whodunnits, I'll put you in the picture about Lemmy Beaglehole. How he murdered the grandson of my dearest friend."

5

BEWARE YUMMY CRUMBY

The Bay View's wine bar, Decant Resist, was as seductive as its name. Earth tones of russet and clay, driftwood accents, and soft recessed lights pulled Jem in. As did a familiar face: Micki Latham, snug in a corner booth with a glass of red wine.

"Jem!" she called, waving.

Detaching herself from Mrs. Jones, Jem hurried to Micki, who jumped up for a hug. Jem had never been one for casual embraces, but the extroverted Micki was as bad as any American. She never missed a chance to shower her friends with affection. And while Jem hadn't been raised to be especially demonstrative, in her secret heart, she kind of liked it.

"Is Pauley with you?"

"Yes, but she's on contest duty. Also, she's checking out the room the Bake Off Committee gave us. Turns out being the Mistress of Ceremonies has its perks."

"Thank goodness. I must have rung and texted you guys a hundred times."

"Did you?" Jem checked her mobile. "There's no missed

calls or messages. Oh—there's no bars, either. Do you have any?"

Micki consulted her phone. "Nope. I reckon service is down. Lord knows when it will be back. Can't believe you were mad enough to let Pauley talk you into coming out here. Was Rhys okay with it?"

Jem waved that away. "What about you? Did Clarence guilt trip you into coming with him as moral support?"

"Worse. I'm here in his place. He decided to stay with the B&B in case there's storm damage," Micki said. "There are guests in residence. He can't leave them on the property alone during an emergency. But he was determined to put his cake in the Bake Off, storm or no storm, because he paid his fee. You know how cheap he can be."

"Frugal," Jem corrected, as Clarence always did when he heard that particular C-word. In his book, cheapness was a sin, but frugality was a virtue.

"Right. Anyway, here I am, Muggins of the Year, drowning my sorrows because I'll probably be stuck overnight. I thought I might have to bed down in this booth. But if you and Pauley have a room, that makes tonight a sleepover. Better yet—a slumber party."

"Too right. So... you know who's judging, don't you?" Jem asked carefully.

"I do." Micki took another sip.

"And you're not bothered?"

"Of course, I'm bothered." Micki ran her fingers through her hair, which was poofier and frizzier than Jem had ever seen it. "Why do you think I look like I stuck my finger in a socket? Even my hair follicles are freaking out. Today was supposed to be Clarence's big moment. He signed up so he could meet Lemmy in person and confront him. Cut him down to size and get some of our own back."

"Cut down Beaglehole? Now that's what I like to hear," Mrs. Jones said, shoehorning herself into the conversation. Jem opened her mouth to make introductions, but the old lady grabbed the wheel.

"I'm Lobelia Jones," she said, shaking Micki's hand vigorously. "Grandmother of one contestant and friend of another. Chief strategist for Bakers Against Beaglehole. Now, what precisely did the little wretch do to you?"

"Ended my singing career with one nasty review," Micki said. "What did he do to you?"

"He murdered Isolde's ex-husband, Trevor Morton, in cold blood."

"But... didn't you just scold her for wearing Trev's mac? Because he might need it in this weather?" Jem asked.

"Oh, his body's still walking around," Mrs. Jones said, waving that away. "But his soul is dead, and I won't rest till I see Beaglehole punished."

As Micki and Mrs. Jones dished over the sins of Lemmy Beaglehole and *All Things Penzance*—the local website that published his infamous hot takes on books, concerts, and restaurants—Jem headed to the counter to order a pot of tea. At least, she managed a few steps in the counter's general direction. Then she found herself at the end of a queue that was fifteen people deep.

But it's only a quarter past eleven, Jem thought. *Guess everyone thinks it's going to be one of those days.*

Behind the counter, Decant Resist's lone employee bravely grappled with the tide of humanity. A freckled ginger of about twenty-five, he appeared personable and well-versed in the various wines on offer. The patrons within earshot were all smiling and nodding, apparently enjoying the ginger's presentation. His tip jar was full of notes.

The queue inched forward. Over in Reception, someone groaned. Jem's head swiveled—after encountering a certain number of corpses in the wild, you become attuned to sounds of pain and distress. But this turned out to be the theatrical groaning of a traveler who didn't like whatever Mr. Fernsby, now ensconced behind the check-in desk, was telling him. Soon, the unhappy man turned shouty. Jem heard something about phone calls, corporate hotlines, and Yelp reviews.

"Throwing a right royal fit," the person queued behind her said. "That'll teach Mother Nature to ground all the helicopters."

"They're officially grounded?" Jem asked, turning.

The speaker, a woman with abundant smile lines, nodded. "The word came while I was outside. Just before that dotty pensioner got up off the carpet. One family who chartered a helicopter had a breakdown. Talk about privilege." She shrugged. "It didn't help that a copter just passed overhead. Probably to make an emergency landing."

"Was it red and white?" Jem asked, thinking of HM Coastguard search and rescue craft.

"No, it was white, I believe. I wondered if the man with the canceled charter would go looking for the pilot and demand to be flown to the mainland. But if he did, I guess it didn't work, because there he is, threatening all the manager holds dear."

"There still could be ferries," Jem said doubtfully, remembering what Bart had said about finding a safe berth. Of all the ferry captains, Bart was the most likely to carry on in iffy weather. If he was sitting out Storm Veronica, they all were. "You know what? Scratch that."

"I'd say most of these people agree with you." The woman nodded at those who'd already been served. "You don't start drinking reds before noon if you expect to soon make a stomach-churning voyage across the Celtic Sea. As for me, I'll nurse a Chardonnay and wait till mid-afternoon. If the weather doesn't improve, I'll rebook my old room."

As the freckled ginger continued his presentations and the queue continued to inch forward, Jem glanced over her shoulder to see how Micki and Mrs. Jones were getting on. They seemed to be chatting amiably. She turned her attention to the common area between Decant Resist and Reception.

It was an airy, welcoming place, carpeted in beige and furnished with overstuffed sofas and club chairs. Dead center was a table bearing cups, napkins, and a huge glass decanter of iced water. The water looked enticing; delicate herbs and yellow lemon slices floated on top. Some of the would-be departees had taken refuge there, including a tired-looking mum and her two children, a boy and girl who were both under ten. As they ran around in circles, threatening each other over possession of a soft toy, their mum stared fixedly up at the ceiling.

Finally, it was Jem's turn. The freckled ginger's name turned out to be Xavier, and his workstation had been personalized beyond that bountiful tip jar. A couple of pithy memes had been printed out and taped to the side of the cash register. And on the counter sat three cunning little *Star Wars* figures, all of them crocheted: Baby Yoda, the Mandalorian, and Darth Vader.

"Did you make those?" she asked, charmed.

"A gift. Now. How can I brighten your day?" Xavier,

who was tall and fit but not handsome, gave Jem a smile that recalibrated his features, making him suddenly compelling. "You seem like a Pinot Gris woman, am I right?"

"Ordinarily, yes, but in this case, I'll just have a pot of tea. With milk, sugar, and three cups."

He looked disappointed. "Sure you don't need something stronger? We're in for a dark and stormy night."

"Then I'll be back for vino later. For the moment, just tea."

"Kind?"

"Caffeinated."

"I suggest a twist on an old favorite. Fifty Shades of Earl Grey. It's strong, heady, and sophisticated. You'll adore it. Just give me a few ticks and you'll be all set."

Nodding her thanks, Jem returned to Micki and Mrs. Jones's booth, only to find they'd attracted company. Near the table hovered a boyish man in his early forties. Tall and slightly stooped, he had floppy brown hair and a mournful expression.

"Oh, lovely, Jem, you're back just in time," Mrs. Jones told her. "This is my grandson-in-law, Trevor Morton. The one I mentioned before? He's here to take part in the Bake Off."

Glutton for punishment, eh? Jem thought, looking him over. Why would he again subject himself to Lemmy's judgment if, as Mrs. Jones put it, his soul had been murdered? He didn't quite fit her idea of a baker. With his big nose, wide mouth, and pointed chin, he seemed more like a generic musician. The unnamed bass player in an unsigned British band, perhaps.

"If you want to be accurate, I'm not her grandson-in-law," Trevor told Jem. "I'm her ex-grandson-in-law." To

Mrs. Jones he added, "Good thing Isolde isn't here. She doesn't like it when you pretend to forget."

"My dear Isolde dislikes a great many things," Mrs. Jones said breezily. "You should have seen her a little while ago. Incandescent with rage. Be a dear and tell Vera, will you?"

"She's having a lie down in our room."

"Bunking here together for the night," Mrs. Jones clarified to Jem and Micki.

"Really? I thought you lived on St. Martin's," Jem said.

"We do. I live with Isolde, in the cottage next door to her shop. Trev and Vera have a little place on the other side of the island. High Town, they call it. When we heard the storm might hit, Vera suggested that the family take a room. Two beds, four people, and one loo. But economical that way."

"Not all family. Not really. And if it wasn't for Isolde, I would've stayed home," Trevor said in his glum way. "It's mental to hold a contest in this weather."

"The way I see it, the fewer the bakers, the better the chance of winning," Micki said.

"I have no chance." Without a goodbye, Trevor trudged away toward the lifts, shoulders slumping.

"Trev! Make Isolde return your mac! Stand up for yourself!" Mrs. Jones called to his back, but he didn't turn around.

Sighing, Mrs. Jones looked from Jem to Micki. "Don't judge him too harshly. He's regressed back into adolescence. The terrible teens. And all because—"

"Hold that thought," Jem interrupted apologetically. Their order had appeared at last on Xavier's long counter.

On her way back to the booth with their trayful of tea things, Jem spied a very wet Hack slink into the lobby from outside. He looked as if he'd gone swimming in his full police kit.

I've never seen him so dejected. Not since he crashed that runabout at Snoggy Cove, anyway. That means the RIB is probably lost. And he'll be riding out the storm here with us.

As she watched, he entered the men's lavatory. Did it contain sufficient paper towels to get a man that wet dry again? Time would tell.

Back in the booth with Micki and Mrs. Jones, Jem played mother, pouring tea and passing around cups as the old woman resumed her story.

"I love Isolde to death. You might not have been able to tell from our little tête-à-tête in the lobby, but I do. And I feel exactly the same about poor Trevor. I might even love him a teensy bit more. He needs me.

"I had a son long ago," Mrs. Jones continued, "but between you, me, and the wall, he didn't work out. Just a bad fit." She shrugged. "It happens like that sometimes in families, though people hate to admit it. Anyway, he left home, tied the knot, untied the knot, and moved to Australia to do heavens knows what. He was too busy to bring up his only daughter properly, so when Isolde was small, I took the reins. She's been with me ever since.

"My friend Vera went through a similar thing with her daughter. Poor girl was forever in rehab or joining a new church or getting deprogrammed. Went to London on a lark and disappeared off the face of the earth. Her grandson Trev was better off with Vera. Lord, the four of us used to have such fun together. Trev and Isolde grew up and fell in love. Married right out of school."

"Too fast?" Micki asked.

"No, of course not. When your heart speaks, why wait?" Mrs. Jones looked at Micki's left hand. "Are you divorced?"

"Proudly single." Micki sipped her tea.

"What about you? I don't see a ring," Mrs. Jones said, pouncing on Jem.

Out of the old lady's line of sight, Micki pretended to scratch her cheek with a certain finger. Jem bit her lip to hold back a laugh.

"I'm divorced, actually," she said. "But never mind that. What happened to Trevor and Isolde? I couldn't help noticing that he corrected you when you failed to call him your ex-son-in-law. Sounded like he was concerned for Isolde's feelings."

"You do pay attention, don't you?" Mrs. Jones said. "Yes, he's always safeguarding her feelings, no matter what it costs him. If she told him the only way she could be happy was for him to cut off his head, he'd build a self-propelled guillotine."

"I'm betting she found him too clingy," Micki said.

"When the going got rough, Isolde became too Isolde and Trevor became too Trevor," Mrs. Jones said. "They were fine at first. Then Trev went off to culinary school at Ilfracombe and the separation was hard on Isolde. When he came back fully qualified and bursting to open his own bakery, she got jealous. Even though she had a good job at Asda—management track—she suddenly gave that up and insisted on attending culinary school, too. Isolde could never bear the idea that someone had something that she didn't.

"I scraped up the fees for Ilfracombe," Mrs. Jones continued. "And off Isolde went. Meanwhile, Trev opened his first bakery in Hugh Town, but couldn't keep it afloat. There's too much entrenched competition on St. Mary's.

Poor boy lost all his seed money trying to make a go of it. He wanted to try again, but Vera couldn't cover the fees for another startup, so I stepped in."

Wondering if Isolde had appreciated the extra help lavished on Trevor or resented it, Jem said, "That was generous of you."

"I was happy to do it. I wanted him to succeed. And even though he was bruised by his failure in Hugh Town, he wasn't crushed. He still had life in him. I convinced him to try the mainland," Mrs. Jones said. "He bought a defunct bakery in Penzance, refurbished it, and he was so hopeful. It was wonderful to see." She smiled fondly. "Isolde promised to help him run it after she graduated. But she never got the chance, because Lemmy Beaglehole dropped in one day and killed Trev with his poison pen."

"I already filled Mrs. Jones in on what happened to me," Micki told Jem. "How I used to carry Lemmy's review of my performance at the Minack Theater around in my bag. I'd have it to this day if Rhys hadn't snatched it away and set it on fire."

"Which is what it deserved," Jem said. The memory of that day gave her a pang. Rhys could be a prize arse when he wanted to, but he could also be a bloody prince. "When are you going to start singing again?"

Pretending not to hear, Micki turned back to Mrs. Jones. "What did Lemmy write about Trevor's pastry? Was it really that bad?"

"It was devastating," Mrs. Jones said, blue eyes glittering. "He exploited Trev's one weakness: the name of his shop. It was a silly name, but he insisted. I couldn't talk him out of it, and neither could his grandmother. He called it Yummy Crumby."

"Crumby as in crumb? Meaning cake?" Micki asked. "I mean—it's not the greatest, but it works, doesn't it?"

"The review was entitled, 'Beware Yummy Crummy: Bad for Your Tummy.' C-r-u-m-m-y, of course," Mrs. Jones said. "The wretched thing got thirty thousand shares on Facebook. Lots of reaction videos from those TikTok ghouls."

"But people say there's no such thing as bad publicity," Jem said.

Mrs. Jones barked a derisive laugh. "After snarking about the upholstery and the paint and the pattern on the coffee cups, Lemmy said Trev's pastry gave him the trots. Diarrhea is never good publicity, and anyone who says otherwise is quite mad.

"What's worse is, Lemmy blamed Trev directly. Called him strange and unpleasant. Said his fingernails were visibly dirty under his clear plastic gloves. A lie," Mrs. Jones cried. "A flat-out lie. Trev always maintained the highest standards of cleanliness. His food never made anyone ill. What's more, his gloves were always blue nitrile. Yes, his hands were clean underneath, but the point is, the fact Lemmy referred to the gloves as clear proves that he never actually saw the state of Trev's fingernails. He just made that up. He rhymed tummy with crummy and concocted a story to support it."

"Sounds like slander," Micki said. "Or do I mean libel?"

"Libel," Jem said. "Couldn't Trevor sue Lemmy for defamation? I think the accused defamer has to prove in court that what they alleged in print is true."

"Yes, he could have," Mrs. Jones said. "But we left it too long. More than anything, Trev wanted his place to succeed. We borrowed money for advertising. He gave away free samples—or tried to. But the word was out. So he lost another bakery." She sighed. "We should have sued Lemmy straight away instead of trying to do damage control. But, if I'm being honest, I'm not sure how good Trev would have been in court. He withdrew. Fell into a deep depression. That's what I meant by him being too Trev. Meanwhile, Isolde was away at college getting attention and becoming ever more full of herself. When they were finally reunited, he clung to her like a drowning man. And all she wanted was to get away."

6

THE MAD POISONER

There seemed to be nothing more to say about Isolde and Trevor's failed marriage, so the three of them lapsed into silence, drinking their tea. Jem let her eyes roam. In Decant Resist, the oenophiles seemed reasonably happy with their wine choices, but in the common area, the travelers were still afflicted by that rowdy brother and sister duo. Having abandoned their custody battle over the stuffie, they were now arguing over candy. Meanwhile, in Reception, the audible discontent was ratcheting up. The man who'd ranted about customer hotlines and Yelp reviews—tall, silver-haired, incongruously distinguished—seemed to be inciting his fellow guests to some kind of action. It sounded like a revolution against Fernsby.

"A woman in the queue told me there was a meltdown over helicopters being grounded. Now what's the problem?" Jem asked.

"Affluenza," Micki said. "Probably never heard the word no before. He keeps insisting he wants off the island and he's gobsmacked that nobody can make it happen."

"Yes, well, the squeaky wheel gets the oil," Mrs. Jones

said. "You wouldn't believe what I've accomplished by complaining. People detest confrontations."

"It didn't work on Pauley," Jem said.

"Yes, but she's a Gwyn. She's not easily buffaloed. A rare quality these days." Mrs. Jones sipped her tea. "Two things I taught Isolde. One, sit back and observe. As a sleuth, I'm sure you agree," she told Jem. "Second, when you want something, demand it. If only I'd instilled the same lessons in Trevor. He would have seen how his clinginess was pushing Isolde away. Instead of kowtowing, he should have demanded she give them a second chance. It would have worked, I know it would."

Hack emerged from the men's room, wet hair combed back and still damp all over. Apparently, there weren't enough paper towels, though at least he was no longer dripping. Still, he looked miserable.

"Poor bloke. Bet he'd give his right hand for a change of clothes," Micki said. "Jem, why don't you invite him up to your room to use the blow dryer?"

"What?"

"Don't look at me like that. It works. When I was short of cash, I used to skip the launderette and blow dry my clothes. Of course, you have to wring them out well, and it takes forever with a jumper or corduroy, but it's better than walking around soaked to the skin."

It sounded like a plan to Jem. But before she could catch Hack's eye and signal for him to come their way, the powder keg in the reception area exploded at last.

"There *must* be a shortwave radio," the silver-haired man thundered. "It would be madness to run a business out in the middle of nowhere without a means of emergency communication." He stabbed a finger at Fernsby, who'd unwisely come out from behind the counter and was now mobbed by angry faces. "If you won't show me where it is, I'll take away your keys and find it myself."

"This is unacceptable," Fernsby cried, sounding terrified. "Sergeant Hackman!"

"I'd hate to do the paperwork on tasering a tourist." Hack's voice, calm but loud, had a dangerous edge. He strolled into Reception with deliberate nonchalance, hands on his duty belt, with all the poise and swagger of a man in dry clothes. "But if you don't stop behaving badly, I'm going to do it. And I might even enjoy it."

The declaration was followed by ringing silence. Hack stared down the silver-haired man. For his part, the silver-haired man seemed completely stunned.

"Do you know who I am?" he said at last.

"Yes. You're a visitor to the Isles of Scilly who just assaulted the manager of this establishment. And he would have every right to have you removed from the premises and banned for life, if the weather outside wasn't a danger to life and limb."

"My name is Sebastian A. Minting," the distinguished man said gravely, as if the mere utterance could force Hack to back down. "I don't respond well to threats."

"Perhaps not, but you deal in them pretty freely. Suppose Mr. Fernsby decides to press charges?"

Hack's deadpan manner cooled the incipient mob. Jem wasn't surprised. Most of them looked like gelatinous types who preferred to have lackeys fight their battles.

"I don't know whether the Bay View has a shortwave or not," Hack continued. "But if you think the coastguard will dance to your tune and send a boat to whisk you to the mainland, you're sorely mistaken. The storm is upon us and no one is leaving here until—"

"False imprisonment," Minting cut across him. "I know

my rights. You can't prevent me and my family from leaving. I saw a helicopter overhead half an hour ago. I think it landed on the other side of the island. There may be ferries waiting there."

"There aren't," Hack shouted. "Look at me. I almost fell in the drink trying to rescue my RIB. The winds are so strong, the mooring line snapped. It was swept out to sea. You're right, I can't compel you to remain here, unless I cuff you to a chair. But if you lead your family outside, you'll all end up tumbling down hills or catching your deaths of cold." He spread his hands. "Listen. Instead of bullying Fernsby, why don't you make nice and rebook your old room? Unless you're comfortable sleeping on the floor with your suitcase for a pillow. Now if you'll excuse me, I could use a drink of water."

With all the dignity he could muster in a sticky-wet uniform, Hack started toward the lemon water decanter. Minting looked dissatisfied, as if he wanted to renew his argument but didn't know which tack to take. Fernsby retreated to safety behind the check-in counter, assisting a marginally more polite gentleman in re-engaging his former suite.

As Hack approached the water decanter, the little girl shrieked.

"No! I'm engaged! No!" With a groan, she tried to pull her hand away from her brother's mouth, now attached to the candy diamond on her finger. "Mum! Make him stop. He always takes my things!"

"I know, I know," said their mother, reluctantly bringing herself to look in her children's direction. "Colin, spit out your sister's ring. Colin. Spit it out. I mean it this time."

Hack, who'd poured himself a cupful of water, took a

drink and smiled at the mum, who asked, "I don't suppose you'd still like to taser someone?"

"That might be a little extreme. How about I cuff your son's hands behind his—" Hack broke off, coughing. "Behind his back. The way things are going, I may have to convert a broom closet into a ..." He coughed again. "A jail..." His face was turning red.

"Don't try to talk," the mum said sympathetically, rising. "Sounds like it went down wrong. We'll leave you in peace. Colin. Emma. Come along. Off to the gift shop."

Taking each child by the hand, she steered them out of the common area and into the corridor that led to the lifts, the gift shop, and the dining room of Kestrel & Peregrine, the Bay View Hotel's two-rosette-award-winning restaurant. "Perhaps they have coloring books and crayons on offer."

As the family departed, Hack was seized by a deeper spasm of coughs. His empty cup fell from his hand. Micki poked Jem. Seeing his scarlet face, she jumped up, alarmed, and ran to him.

She meant to give him a good pounding on the back, but when she reached Hack's side, she realized he wasn't choking on anything. He was simply having trouble drawing breath. Meanwhile, his skin was breaking out in angry, expanding welts.

"Hack, say something!"

His fingers dug under his collar, which suddenly looked as tight as a tourniquet. He managed to loosen his tie, but it gave no relief. He couldn't speak. When he opened his mouth, only a thin, whistling sound came out.

His airway is swelling shut!

Wildly she looked around the room for the first aid kit. There should have been a red and white box affixed to the wall, probably near a fire extinguisher. But Jem saw nothing of the sort. Only bland hotel art and a small gold plate bearing directions to the lifts.

"I need the first aid kit," Jem shouted at Fernsby's assistant, she of the premonition and the ill-fitting suit. "Where is it?"

She only gaped at her, mute.

Whirling, Jem found herself face to face with Micki, who'd followed her to Hack's side. Mrs. Jones watched anxiously from their booth.

"What can I do?"

"Get the manager," Jem ordered, making a dash for Decant Resist. Xavier, halted in the process of pouring a glass, stood frozen behind the counter, transfixed by Hack's distress.

"First aid kit!" Jem shouted at him. "Where is it?"

He blinked. "Um. First. I'm not meant to give out hotel gear to guests. Second. I'm not sure—"

"You must have one," she interrupted, knocking over the crocheted *Star Wars* figures as she invaded his mini sanctum. On the other side of the counter lay the secrets of his work universe: his mobile phone, some boating magazines, half a sandwich, and a big plastic case divided into individual square compartments. Thinking she'd hit pay dirt, Jem seized it.

"Oi!" Xavier looked shocked.

"Hey! That's my personal property!" cried Fernsby's assistant, mute no longer.

Barely registering either of them, Jem snapped the case's latches and lifted the lid. What she saw inside was a mass of red, white, pink, green, blue, and purple shapes. Her stunned brain tried to impose order, turning them into medical supplies. Pills, maybe?

"You have no right." Xavier seized the case, tugging hard. Bits and bobs flew into the air, clattering down again in a hard-plastic rain.

Beads, Jem realized. Barrels, rounds, briolettes, and rondelles, pattering down her shirt and across the floor. Rounding on Xavier, who was tall enough to look her in the eye, she grabbed him by the shoulders and yelled, "Give me the real kit!"

Jerking out of her grasp, he flailed around under the cash register, tossed aside a rubbish bin, and emerged with a red and white box. Speechless at the idiocy of stashing it in such a place, Jem snatched it away and ran back to Hack. He was on the floor, still struggling to breathe, lips swollen, eyes wide. She'd never seen him so frightened. Not even close.

"Get back!" Jem bellowed at the onlookers, though it was hardly necessary. No one was doing anything except watching and wringing their hands.

"Don't worry, Hack. It's going to be all right," Jem said, dropping to her knees beside him. The welts on his cheeks stood out horribly. His chest strained mightily, but the only respiratory sound was a faint whistle.

The kit's seals broke with a loud *crack*. Inside were bandages, gauze, disinfectant, scissors, tweezers, a tourniquet...

With a cry of relief, Jem pounced on the adrenaline autoinjector. Popping the cap, she raised the instrument. But when she tuned back to Hack, her mind went blank.

Where do I administer it?

Hack slapped the widest part of his thigh. Feeling like an idiot, Jem jammed the sterile needle in, right through his trousers.

How soon will it take effect? What do I do in the meantime?

Still holding the autoinjector in place, she studied the instrument, wondering if she'd bungled the application. Was there a plunger to push? There didn't seem to be one. How could she be sure the medicine had deployed properly?

Just when she'd nearly convinced herself to pull out the needle and try again, Hack's hand closed over hers. Their eyes met, and suddenly she understood.

I don't have to do anything else. Just hold it in place, she thought, her long-ago health and safety training flooding back to her at last. *If I hadn't gone to pieces over those ruddy beads, I might have taken two seconds to read the instructions. They're printed all over the package.*

Hack took a breath that was slightly deeper, if still whistling. She could tell by the look in his eyes that he wasn't panicking anymore. Suddenly, neither was she.

For what seemed like a long time the two of them were frozen in place, their hands clasped around the autoinjector. Slowly but surely, the whistling grew fainter, then abated altogether. Each breath he took seemed to come easier. Then his swollen lips parted, and he croaked, "Pull it out."

Gradually, Hack improved. First, he sat up. Then, with Jem's help, he stood up. The effort triggered another fit of hard, pained coughing. Alarmed, Jem steered him over to a club chair.

"It's... okay..." he gasped. "If I'm coughing, I'm breathing."

Jem nodded sympathetically. The hives on his cheeks were still elevated and scarlet, but at least his cheeks and neck seemed to have deflated a little.

A hand fell on Jem's shoulder. She jumped, but it was

only Micki. She had the manager, Fernsby, in tow. Most of the rubberneckers had backed off, but Mrs. Jones had entered the common area. Standing on tiptoe, she peered curiously into the water decanter.

"Yes. Well. It seems like everything's in order now. Good show, everyone. A-okay," Fernsby announced. There was a hollow quality to his voice and a faint mist on his spectacle lenses. Apparently, the confrontation with Minting had taken its toll.

"Okay isn't the word I'd use," Jem said. "Hack was fine until he drank a cup of that water. And why was the first aid kit hidden? It should have been in plain sight." She shot a glance at Decant Resist, where Xavier stood glaring at her. Instead of explaining himself, he pointedly turned away, taking refuge in his queue, which was reforming post-incident.

"Maybe the Mad Poisoner's to blame," Mrs. Jones suggested. She served herself a small amount of water, sniffing it rather than drinking it.

"Mad—" Fernsby broke off. "I really must insist that no one use that phrase in conjunction with this establishment," he said testily. "Besides, haven't you caused enough trouble, Mrs. Jones?"

"I'm not the one responsible for this water, now am I?"

"What do you mean, Mad Poisoner?" Jem asked.

"King Triton's," Micki said. "Has to be."

Jem felt as if she were losing the plot. "What are you two on about?"

"There used to be a seafood shack here on St. Martin's called King Triton's," Micki said. "It went kaput. Bad seafood."

"And after it closed, Isolde and I bought it. It's now Cake Me Proud," Mrs. Jones chimed in. "There was a rash of food poisonings last summer. No one died, but it got so bad, folks were afraid to eat there. The Mad Poisoner was never caught."

"The Mad Poisoner never existed." Fernsby still sounded huffy. "Food poisoning happens in poorly managed restaurants. And seafood is notoriously tricky to maintain at safe temperatures. It was a silly panic caused by idle gossip."

"If there's no Mad Poisoner, how do you explain what happened to Mr. Policeman?" Mrs. Jones asked sweetly.

"Perhaps he's allergic."

"To water?"

Fernsby turned away from her. Over at Decant Resist, the queue was fifteen deep again, and Xavier had regained his equilibrium, smiling and joking with patrons as if Hack hadn't nearly asphyxiated. Jem wanted to slap him. Didn't he realize what might have happened?

As for the ponytailed clerk, she was on her hands and knees, gathering beads. With the case open by her side, she was picking them up in ones and twos, carefully depositing them back into their correct compartments. At the rate she was going, when she finished, Storm Veronica would be but a memory.

"Agnetha," Fernsby called. "Sweep up that rubbish and come back to Reception. Everyone's re-booking and I need your help."

"But I—"

"Now." Fernsby's voice cracked. He must have been breathing hard because his specs were fogging up.

Lightning flashed outside the foyer's glass doors, bold and brilliant. A soft *ahhh* went through the room. The requisite boom of thunder that followed was so loud, chandeliers tinkled and a ripple of nervous laughter passed through the Bay View's reluctant guests.

"Jem." Micki squeezed her forearm. "What's happening over there?"

She pointed down the corridor. By the lifts, Jem saw a tall person wearing a flapping brown overcoat and a floppy pink sun hat open the door marked STAIRS and disappear through it.

"That's weird," Jem said, but Micki didn't hear her. A cataclysmic boom of thunder drowned everything out, prompting gasps from everyone. When the vibrations peaked, the Bay View Hotel went black. Dead black.

7

PAULEY GWYN, MISTRESS OF MACABRE CEREMONIES

"Mod-cons," Pauley Gwyn hummed to herself as she floated through her second floor, garden view room. "Magical, glorious mod-cons."

Although she was quite alone in the room—Jem was on the ground floor, presumably still having tea with Mrs. Jones—Pauley narrated the tour to an imaginary audience.

"As you see, simplicity is one of my favorite virtues," she said, pausing to indicate the bedside lamp and table combination. "Simplicity is the cornerstone of a gracious home. White on white with soft curves and clean lines. Don't you love how beautifully it harmonizes with these thousand-thread-count sheets? Never apologize for luxury. Make your bed with linens that invite you to sleep in nothing at all."

Giggling, she moved on to the desk, which was stocked with Bay View Hotel engraved stationery and envelopes. "Feeling a touch Mary Shelley? Pick up a pen and spill marvelous words all over the page. My fingers *never* touch a keyboard. When I write, I indulge in the joy of longhand correspondence." She paused, considering. "Nope, scrub that, I'd sooner send a text. What I *mean* to say is, isn't it lovely to sit at a desk and pensively gaze out at the storm?"

She pushed aside the curtains and peeked out. Storm Veronica glared back malignantly, still hovering over the water but much closer now. "Yikes." Pauley let the curtain drop. "Well, let's pretend that was a gorgeous view of my expertly manicured lawn and garden. Fret over crumbling walls and broken gates? Not I. My staff of well-compensated, shockingly attractive gardeners attend to all my landscaping needs."

That bit of wish fulfillment made her laugh. The grounds of Lyonesse House were many things, but manicured wasn't one of them. After opening and closing all the drawers, peering into the closet, examining the electric kettle, and snapping a selfie by a flower arrangement, Pauley entered the room's crown jewel, the bathroom.

"In my gracious home," she told her imaginary audience, "I rely on the very best in reliable modern plumbing. Note the sink's *single-handle* waterfall faucet." She demonstrated turning it on and off, marveling in its efficiency. "Of course, in very old, very tedious homes, you'll find two spouts—one for hot water, one for cold. If you want warm water, you must run them both at once and sort of frantically splash the streams together. The finest technology 1850 had to offer!"

Imaginary tour completed, she returned to the window to watch the storm. She knew what Rhys would be doing right now, assuming he wasn't deep in a sulk over his row with Jem. He was up on his lighthouse's observation deck, palette loaded with indigo and ebony, painting nature's fury. She looked forward to seeing Storm Veronica through his eyes. Though he paid the bills with his sunsets, moody storms inspired some of his best work.

The room phone trilled. Pauley looked at it suspiciously, wondering who it could be. In the halls she'd glimpsed a few vendors, as well as a couple of Bake Off contestants, but no other committee members. She was probably the only one fool enough to come and see the festival through.

What if it's Lemmy?

She hadn't willingly spoken to him in over fifteen years, but like a bad penny, he occasionally turned up, or sent her a text out of the blue. He seemed to be under the impression she was carrying a torch for him. It made her skin crawl.

She snatched up the receiver. "Yes?"

"Don't you sound cross. I'm intrigued," said Pranav Dhillon. "Has the weather put you in a temper?"

Sagging with relief, Pauley eased down on the bed, which she found supremely comfortable. "Well, it's not the best, obvs. But we're here now and at least I have a nice room. How's it looking in Penzance?"

The line crackled loudly. "I'm actually in the islands." Pranav's voice sounded muddy, as if coming from the other side of the world. "It's pitch-black and the wind's howling. I couldn't get through to your mobile, so I decided to try your room..." He faded out.

"The islands? What are you doing here?"

Silence.

"Pranav, can you hear me?"

"... flew over and landed just in time..."

"Pranav, you're breaking up. Can you hear me?" Although he was a professional helicopter pilot, she couldn't believe he'd dared fly over the Celtic Sea with a storm on the horizon. When he wasn't giving aerial tours, he occasionally flew chartered trips from Penzance to Tresco, but only in good weather. Someone must had offered him bags of cash to take such a risk. And while she certainly understood the temptation, she didn't approve.

"I can hear you," Pranav said, now sounding like he was calling from Mars. "I know I shouldn't have done it, but greed won out. If I'm ever going to save up enough for us to be together, I have to take every fare."

It made sense. Pranav was in the midst of a weird but blessedly amicable divorce from his wife, Nora. They'd fallen out of love and decided to split up, but the bad economy had left them chained to a home they couldn't sell and couldn't walk away from. Until they managed to find a buyer, they were still cohabiting, albeit as roommates.

"I just need to know that you're safe. Where are you?"

"Oh, I'm safe. Don't freak out, but—"

The line cut out. No dial tone. Only silence.

Groaning, Pauley did that thing people in old movies do, hitting the switch hook several times, as if that would magically restore the connection. It didn't.

She wasn't worried about Pranav's safety, not really, but she wished he could have finished his sentence. What did he mean, don't freak out? Had he crash landed the helicopter? Was he calling from St. Mary's Hospital?

Outside, a tongue of white lightning split the sky. On its heels came a clap of thunder that rattled the bulbs in the wall sconces.

Stop it. He's fine. He can take care of himself.

It was a shame he wasn't on St. Martin's, so they could weather the storm together. Their relationship had turned serious around Christmas, and now she couldn't wait for him to get his divorce decree. (Neither could Nora, who had a boyfriend of her own and was equally ready to move on.) Not just because they could finally start making plans, but because then she could finally tell the second most important man in her life, Rhys, that Pranav existed.

Ever since their schooldays, Rhys had appointed himself Pauley's protector, whether she liked it or not. Sometimes, as in the case of fortune hunters who believed her trust fund to be bigger than it was, she was happy to have Rhys chase them away. But most of the time, she found the big blond gorilla exasperating. She wasn't about to subject Pranav to Rhys at his worst.

After all, Jem and Micki had found it hard enough to accept that Pauley was dating a technically married man. *And* he was still cohabitating with his spouse. They now accepted Pranav's sincerity, but Rhys... there were parts of his brain that were indistinguishable from Early Man. Cave dwellers from the Paleolithic would probably respond to Rhys's overprotective big brother act with, "Dude. Chill." She knew he'd been sniffing around and had managed to learn she occasionally visited a helicopter pilot on the mainland. Pauley had covered herself by claiming that pilot's name was Felix Catchpole and he was seventy years old. Once Pranav was a free man, she'd find a way to tell Rhys the truth.

Another boom of thunder rolled through the hotel, making her ears ring. The lights snuffed. Pauley was alone in the dark.

She groped for her mobile. Although a brick in most respects, it still served as a torch. That blue-white beam allowed her to find the door and peer into the hall, where she saw several lights bobbing, like the ghost-orbs of Androids and iPhones.

"This is ghastly," said a woman in an RP accent so starched, it could have chipped ice. "Heaven knows when we'll get power back, here among the primitives."

Pauley caught her breath, but before she could think up a suitable reply, the man at the end of the hall said plaintively, "I have a CPAP machine. How am I meant to sleep?"

A hum rose from somewhere nearby. Slowly, the lights came back on, dimmer than before, but steady.

"Will you look at that?" Pauley smiled at her fellow lodgers. "Generator power. Score one for us primitives."

After that mic drop and the glares that followed, Pauley decided it was time to haul her box down to Ballroom A and finish decorating for the Bake Off. Probably it should have been canceled, and perhaps the Bay View Hotel's captive audience would prove too haughty to even watch. But the show *would* go on, and as Mistress of Ceremonies, she would give it her all.

Taking a lift seemed ill-advised, at least until the generator's efficacy had been proven, so Pauley took the stairs. Halfway down, she ran into one of the contestants, Camille Carlisle.

Camille, a relative newcomer to St. Mary's, had moved to the Scillies after her divorce, and changed her hair color almost as often as Pauley's young friend Kenzie. But while Kenzie seemed intent on working her way through all the colors of the rainbow, Camille stuck to variations of her favorite color, pink. In the past, she'd rocked fuchsia, rose, salmon, and coral. Today it was bubblegum pink, with lipstick and nail polish to match.

"Hiya, Pauley," Camille said cheerily. "I heard you're here with Jem Jago. Tell me, is she working on the stolen crab pots caper?"

"I'm sorry?"

"The stolen crab pots. In Hugh Town," Camille said, as if referencing the crime of the century. "I'm on it. I have a real aptitude. So, tell her she'd better not muscle in on my territory, or else." She flashed a grin. "Kidding! Say, I know it's probably *verboten*, technically at least, but can we talk strategy about the Bake Off? I was wondering—"

"Can't," Pauley said, hurrying on. "Running late, sorry."

No sooner had she escaped one contestant anxiously looking for a last-minute leg-up, than she ran into two more on the ground floor: the husband-and-wife duo of Keir and Posh Darden, who'd paused under a landscape painting to indulge in one of their legendary rows.

After making a modest splash in Cornish local TV, Keir and Posh had retired to St. Mary's in their early fifties. Keir, the former on-air talent, had reinvented himself as an amateur baker, while Posh, a behind-the-scenes producer, served as his cake icing artist. Every year they entered as one, lost as one, and turned on each other multiple times along the way. They seemed to believe it was a case of casting pearls before swine, and if they ever found the right judge, their special genius would finally be recognized. Fortunately, they never asked Pauley what she thought the problem was, or she would have been sorely tempted to tell the truth.

Keir was one of those healthy recipe doctors who couldn't do a classic scone recipe without making it sugarless, fatless, and saltless, all the while insisting it was "just as good, if not better." As for Posh, she was a competent decorator, but naturally Keir insisted she play by his rules, and that meant working with frosting that was gritty or tasteless. In Pauley's view, they needed to find a Bake Off that only permitted slimming recipes and stop competing against the traditional fare done by the Isles of Scilly's finest.

As she tried to hurry past, eyes straight ahead like a woman on a mission, Posh whined, "But it's risky."

"Keep your voice down," Keir whispered harshly.

"Pauley Gwyn! I knew you were made of sterner stuff than to let a little weather keep you home."

"That's right," she said, forcing herself to turn and acknowledge the couple.

"So glad you passed by. Posh and I were just discussing the judge. He doesn't have the best rep, now does he?" Keir flashed his on-air grin, the one that probably snagged the hearts of pensioners up and down the coast. "Any tips?"

"Your cake's already baked. Now's the time for faith," she said, moving on before Posh, whose mouth was open to speak, could further engage her. Posh loved to pull innocent bystanders into her marital dramas, and Pauley had no intention of playing love guru.

She made it to the putative vendor hall, Ballroom B, and looked inside. It was tragic: a slew of empty tables and three vendors. Of course, given the attitude of Bay View's trapped guests, it was probably just as well. She couldn't imagine the lady with the starched accent buying local honey or a knitted muffler.

Ballroom A, beautifully appointed in the Bay View Hotel's signature colors of silver and dusty rose, had already been pre-set by the hotel staff. Clearly, they'd recognized the reality of how small the audience would be; the red curtain she'd requested as a backdrop had been hung in the middle of the ballroom, effectively cutting the huge space in half.

Before the curtain was a raised dais with the judging table. Around the dais, tables and chairs were arranged to seat the audience. An easel board sign welcomed guests to the 17th Annual Valentine's Day Bake Off at the Bay View Hotel. The rest of the decorations were up to her.

Pauley opened her box and got to work. After blowing up pink and white balloons and pinning up red crepe banners, she prettied up the seating area with white linen tablecloths and red posies. She was just adding the final touches—wall posters bearing the names and photos of past winners—when someone said, "Well, well, well. Looks like it's just you and me, Gwyn."

Pauley stiffened. The sound of Lemmy's voice still put her teeth on edge. But she was determined not to let him see how much he got under her skin.

"Hiya, Lems. If you want to be of help, go tell Fernsby the microphone's wonky. We need a working sound system before we can get started."

"I'm sure you can handle that," said Lemmy, who'd never been big on helping. "Turn around and face me. I don't bite. Not unless you want me to."

With a sigh, Pauley forced herself to turn around. When they'd dated as teens, Lemmy's tapered face, high cheekbones, and jutting chin had perfectly suited his spiky black hair and powdered pallor. He'd had a flair for gothic wardrobe, too—all black, in keeping with his alter ego, the Thin Jet Duke.

Of course, living in the Isles of Scilly and Penzance, a wild night of goth clubbing necessitated a rail journey to Bristol, so Lemmy had mostly been the Thin Jet Duke in his head—and to be fair, the occasional online chat room. But Pauley hadn't minded. In those days, Lemmy had been fun, earnest, and good at listening. It wasn't until he decided to de-gothify himself and "get serious," as he put it, that his personality had changed for the worse. He'd become serious, all right—serious, self-important, and addicted to talking up the new Lemmy. It was a crashing bore, and they'd gone their separate ways.

Now, fifteen years later, Lemmy looked exactly like what he was: the most vitriolic, impossible-to-please critic the West Country had ever known. Spawned by online culture, his barbs sharpened by posting daily complaints about the various actors, authors, and musicians that were failing him, he'd become someone who was read by many and liked by none. At least as far as Pauley could tell. She certainly had no intention of ever admitting they'd once dated. Not even Rhys knew.

"Look at you," Lemmy said, smiling in what he probably thought was an ingratiating manner. "Mistress of Ceremonies. Mistress of *Macabre* Ceremonies, if I'm being honest, but I guess some things never change. So tell me, why are you still flogging the goth horse? You'd look gorg as a blonde. A blonde in head-to-toe pastels? Even better."

"If that's how you'd prefer me, I'll be sure to stay spooky. See you around, Lems." She made for the door.

"Oh, come on," he cried, following her. "We have such chemistry. How'd we let it slip away?"

"As I recall, you broke up with me to date your new boss's daughter. Right around the time you binned your eyeliner and gave away your vampire frock coat. In other words," she concluded without heat, "you evolved, and so did I. Now if you'll excuse me, I need to see about a new microphone."

"I heard you took a room," he called as she exited. "I tried to get one, but the stranded emmets snapped them up. I'll need a place to sleep tonight. Bake Off bigwigs should stick together, don't you think?"

She didn't look back, just smiled and walked faster.

8

LOST-AND-FOUND

To Jem's relief, the lights came back on, slightly dimmer and accompanied by a faint hum, after only a couple of minutes. Looking around, she was relieved to find no fresh corpse on the common-room floor. After years of mystery novels, that felt like a bonus.

"Generator?" she asked Fernsby.

"Of course. No expenses were spared when the Bay View was built."

"How long can it run?"

"Three days. Long enough to last out the storm. Now if you'll excuse me..."

Jem grabbed his arm. "Aren't you forgetting something?"

"What?"

"Him." She pointed at Hack, exasperated. His breathing was back to normal, thank goodness, but the hives had yet to fade away, and he was shivering. Sitting around in wet clothes probably didn't help. "What's in that decanter besides water?"

"Ice. Lemon. Sprigs of... sprigs. Agnetha," he called to

the clerk, who had resumed sweeping up quite slowly, perhaps still trying to group the scattered beads with precise broom strokes. "What's that green stuff?"

"Basil."

"Anything else?"

"Nope."

Jem couldn't help noticing that the young woman answered while barely looking their way. The guests who'd witnessed Hack's collapse were still eyeballing him, transparently wondering if he were really out of the woods. Yet Agnetha kept her back to Hack. Maybe seeing a man recovering from near-fatal anaphylaxis was too uncomfortable for her. Or maybe she found her scattered plastic beads more compelling than a man's life.

"Is she responsible for filling the water decanter?" Jem asked Fernsby.

"Yes. Or if not her, someone from the kitchen staff. What does it matter? Sergeant Hackman's probably allergic to lemon."

"I'm not," Hack said weakly.

"Basil, then."

Hack shook his head.

Jem said, "Mr. Fernsby, can I speak to you in private?"

His eyes widened. "Certainly not. Look at Reception. There's still an avalanche of guests who need me."

"They're not going anywhere. Please. Unless you want to talk about the Mad Poisoner," she hissed, "in the open where anyone can overhear?"

"Fine. My office," he said, turning on his heel and leading her straight toward the sea of mutinous faces crowding the check-in desk.

It was like running the gauntlet. Some people moved reluctantly; others remained planted and had to be elbowed aside. An angry man grabbed Fernsby by the coat and Jem had to help pull him free. And at the head of the mob waited none other than Sebastian A. Minting, the tall and distinguished traveler who'd threatened to march his family into the storm in search of a ferry. His face was dead white. Had the brief blackout unnerved him so much?

"Fernsby," he said. "Why haven't you summoned medical help for Sergeant Hackman?"

"Because I can't." Fernsby sounded genuinely amazed by Minting's obtuseness. "We're cut off until the storm ends."

"But that could be hours. Hackman could have died."

"Yes. Well. Let's all be thankful that he didn't." Somehow, Jem and Fernsby reached the door marked NO ADMITTANCE BEYOND THIS POINT. Once they were on the other side of it, he turned the deadbolt.

"You know, Mr. Fernsby, I'm starting to understand the appeal of a nice, wide column."

"This is nothing. They'll be positively monstrous once phone service is restored. I'll be lucky to keep my job."

The windowless office was quite small, no amenities in sight, but at least the walls shielded them from angry faces. Retreating behind his desk, Fernsby sat down and put his chin in his hands and regarded Jem balefully. "Now. What precisely do you want?"

"I want to know what's going on with your employees," Jem said, taking a seat opposite him. "Starting with Agnetha, the girl with all the beads. She didn't seem especially concerned about what happened to Hack."

"I'd say she was in shock. And irritated at Xavier, obviously, for nicking her bead box. Which I've told her to keep in the staff dormitory, not in the hotel proper."

"Dormitory?"

"We're too remote for day employees. Staff live on-site." Fernsby closed his eyes and began to massage his temples. "I work three months on, two weeks off. My staff work two weeks on, one week off. They share a dormitory, or as they call it, a bunkhouse. All personal items, like handheld games, are to be stored there. Agnetha had a bad habit of stringing together beaded necklaces under the counter at check-in. I understand the desire to keep one's hands busy during the down times, but it's not appropriate. I reckon Xavier swiped the box from her to teach her a lesson."

"Okay. Well, shock or no shock, I thought her behavior seemed off. Given what Mrs. Jones said about poisonings at King Triton's—"

"Food poisonings. Bad seafood," Fernsby broke in.

"—it seems like Agnetha should have been a bit keener to assure me the water was safe."

"Why? It is safe." As if heeding his own call to busy his hands, Fernsby reached behind his desk and came up with a large cardboard box marked LOST-AND-FOUND. He began to root through the items, which included a Barbie, a man's patchwork driving cap, and a skein of yarn with a crafting needle stuck in it.

"That's new," he murmured, replacing the yarn in favor of a single wireless earbud. "But back to the water. Come to think of it, I drank some of it myself, first thing this morning. No ill effects, as you can see. And I observed several guests do the same."

"But might someone have doctored the water? Slipped something in at some point?"

"Without being noticed? I don't see how. Only a rather tall person could get the lid off without a step ladder. Unless you're imagining cloak-and-dagger stuff. Wiping an invisible film of poison across the lip of a cup, that sort of thing."

"I can honestly say invisible poison never crossed my mind." As Jem watched, he turned the box over and dumped the remaining contents out on his desk. "Are you looking for something in particular?"

"What? Oh. I just see this box every day. I've come to know every item inside it," Fernsby said, beginning to load it up again. "But a hat and a hooded jacket have gone missing. The owner must have turned up."

Jem suddenly recalled the curious figure of the ragged man—she assumed it was a man—entering the stairwell just before the lights went out. She didn't recall a hoodie, but his flapping brown coat stood out in her memory, and the floppy hat was simply bizarre.

"The missing hat. Is it pink straw? Meant for a lady?"

"How'd you know that?"

"I saw someone wearing it near the lifts," Jem said, and explained in full. Fernsby looked nonplussed.

"Is it a problem?"

"Well, Bay View's open to the public while the restaurant and wine bar are open. After they close, it's guests only," he said. "But the person you described doesn't sound like our sort of clientele. And it seems he may have entered my office and helped himself to a hat."

"I suppose there's more than one pink sun hat in the islands."

"Yes. But there was an unclaimed brown coat in the employee cloakroom. It's been hanging on the peg all winter. Huge and patched and looking as if it belonged to Hagrid. No idea where it came from. Sounds as if the man you saw took that coat, too."

Jem turned it over in her mind. "I know your hotel's

very posh, not to mention remote," she said, "but the islands have always had a little trouble with folks just wandering about, sleeping rough. They come over from the mainland sometimes and think they can hang about, panhandling and island hopping. Hack usually tracks them down and explains it's not allowed. It's sad, really. Do you think perhaps a rough sleeper was wandering St. Martin's and ducked in out of the storm?"

Fernsby finished refilling the box. "It could be. But I don't like the thought of them entering my hotel without making themselves known. Especially if they're sneaking into my office and helping themselves to..." He tailed off.

"Your rubbish?"

"Items that guests have lost and may want back someday."

"Do other employees come and go in here?"

"No, it's always locked. Well, I gave our chef de cuisine a key, but she works too hard to ever use it. And I trust her completely, of course. If she removed items from the lost-and-found, it was for a good reason." He went back to rubbing his temples. "Is there anything else, Ms. Jago?"

"Yes. Your man at Decant Resist, Xavier. What sort of person is he? When I ordered tea, he seemed friendly enough. But when I needed the first aid kit to save Hack's life, he wouldn't give it to me. He didn't seem concerned at all. I practically had to threaten him before he took it out of hiding."

"What? Impossible."

"It's true. Xavier had stashed it under his counter. Behind the rubbish bin, I think. And had the nerve to give me some nonsense about not being able to hand over hotel property."

"Well, he was probably in shock, just like Agnetha. Not

everyone can solve mysteries and take on killers." To her surprise, Fernsby actually smiled. "You have quite a reputation. If I thought anything sinister was actually going on here, I'd be the first person to ask for your help. But Agnetha and Xavier are just..." He tailed off again. "Unexemplary employees, let us say. She's young and still finding her feet. He's outstanding with anyone who might tip him and indifferent to everyone else."

"Right. Well. I don't know what to think just yet, Mr. Fernsby. And I'd better get back to my friends. Hack needs to dry off and everyone needs a break before the Bake Off starts." Jem rose. "Are you coming out or staying in here?"

"I need another minute," he said, eyes sliding back to the lost-and-found box. "Do me a favor, Ms. Jago. If you see that ragged person—interloper, rough sleeper, whatever— try and bring him to me. Until the storm lifts, we're effectively locked down. I insist on knowing the name and face of any suspicious person."

And so do I, Jem thought.

9

KILLER SWEETNESS

At thirty minutes to showtime, Pauley returned with a working microphone in hand to find half of Ballroom A's tables full. For a moment her heart sang—carrying on with the Bake Off wasn't for naught, some people were actually interested. Then she realized that the guests seemed to regard the ballroom as a sort of thwarted traveler clubhouse. The chief agitator among them, Sebastian A. Minting, sat at one table beside what appeared to be his wife and sons. The wife looked distinctly unhappy, as did the younger son. The elder son, who was definitely of age, sat with his eyes closed and his face relaxed, perhaps approaching Zen enlightenment.

Seeing Pauley's frown, one of the thwarted informed her, "We've annexed this area for the duration. The room next door is empty. Move your little shindig there."

"That's impossible. This venue is bought and paid for." Pauley's tone was pure killer sweetness. "Storm Veronica can rage all she wants, but the Valentine's Day Bake Off is happening as scheduled."

"That's ridiculous. No one gives a fig about—"

"Bought and paid for," Pauley cut across the man. "Surely that's a concept near and dear to your heart. But don't leave on our account. Stay and enjoy the competition. Sample the cakes afterward. It's better than squatting in the wine bar and watching the minutes tick by."

Scowling, the man stood up, compelled his significant other to follow with a meaningful glare, and stalked out. A few others followed. Pauley, refusing to be daunted, took to the dais as if everything was hearts and flowers. By the time she finished greeting the bakers, who'd queued up to surrender their cake boxes into her custody, she glanced out and saw all the seats were full again.

As stipulated by the rules, the bakers had written their names across the top of each box. Pauley pushed the curtain backdrop aside, revealing a pie trolley provided by the Bay View's kitchen staff, and began loading it with entries. First came Trevor Morton's white cake box with T. MORTON printed on the lid. Next came Mrs. Vera Lynn Morton's entry in an identical box, with her name in curling script. Third was Isolde's, which arrived in a beautifully decorated Cake Me Proud container.

"Oh, isn't that fancy?" Pauley accepted Camille Carlisle's tall and unusually heavy entry, concealed within a pink decoupage box. "Must be a trifle."

"Yes. In my mum's Godinger Dublin Crystal bowl, no less," Camille said. "Careful."

"Noted. Hiya, Micki," Pauley said, accepting Clarence's entry. It was in an absurdly stylish black and gold box—typical Clarence—and would probably be delicious, assuming he hadn't overdone the exotic ingredients.

As everyone in the islands knew, Clarence was her business partner—at his B&B's darkest hour, she'd stepped in to invest—which was one of the reasons she was Mistress of

Ceremonies, not judge. Even in a blind tasting, it wasn't unreasonable to assume that Pauley might recognize a friend's handiwork. And after a lifetime in the Isles of Scilly, she knew almost every other baker's work, too. Camille, being new to the islands, was the only wild card.

"Where's Jem and Hack?" she asked Micki after another quick glance at the audience. Hack in his copper kit and six-foot-plus and Jem with her double buns were hard to miss.

"Up in the room, still blow drying, I reckon. His trousers are made of heavy stuff. But they'll be here any minute."

"Ta-da! Your winning entry," announced Keir, striding up like Napoleon after the Battle of Austerlitz. His wife Posh trailed a few steps behind, frowning nonspecifically. Maybe she considered herself the loser of their last skirmish.

"Thanks, Keir. Posh. Best of luck," Pauley said, trying to sound like she meant it. "All right, ducks, queue up against that wall. Once I've done a bit more housekeeping, we'll get started." With that, she disappeared behind the red curtain.

Away from prying eyes, she unboxed the desserts, making a list of each type of dessert along with the baker's initials. Then she read through the contestants' bios, the better to read them aloud with confidence. Everyone had submitted one except Clarence. Was it possible Micki had forgotten to bring it?

"Micks," she hissed, peeking around the curtain. "Get over here."

As her friend hurried forth, Pauley checked the audience again. Still a sea of unfriendly faces; still no Jem or Hack. It took a few minutes for them to brainstorm a bio for Clarence. When Pauley looked up again, she was relieved to see Jem entering the room at long last. As her friend took a chair from the extras stacked against the wall, Hack stationed himself by the door as if providing security for the event. He now looked one hundred percent dry, she was pleased to see, even if he only looked fifty percent well. Why didn't he sit down and watch like a normal person? Apparently, you could take the copper out of the job, but you couldn't take the job out of the copper.

"We're ready to kick off," Pauley told the anxious bakers. "Has anyone seen Lemmy?"

"Back there. With the entries." Camille pointed behind the curtain.

"Oh, my lord." Rushing around the flimsy barrier, Pauley discovered Lemmy beside the trolley, blatantly reading her notes.

"What do you think you're doing? You know this is meant to be a blind judging," she whispered angrily.

"Oh, please. It's a Bake Off, not the BAFTAs."

She snatched away the paper with dessert types and names. "Did you memorize my list of who baked what?"

"I might have done." Grinning insolently, he held up a white-streaked finger. "Did a couple of previews, too."

"You're the worst. Wipe that off," she ordered, handing him a napkin. "Right. Now go stand beside the contestants and don't say another word until I introduce you."

"Have you given any more thought to me sharing your room?"

"Not another word."

Clutching her notes, Pauley waited until her heart stopped hammering quite so fiercely. Then, feeling very much like a prize fool, she stepped around the curtain and welcomed her captive audience to the 17th Annual Valentine's Day Bake Off.

Her opening remarks about the importance of culinary skills, which she'd taken great pains to compose, received blank looks. Although she tried to reassure herself that it was going well, she heard her own voice growing squeakier as her delivery came faster and faster. Thank goodness for Jem, the only person who cheered her on, both literally and figuratively.

With the introduction thankfully complete, Pauley moved on to the bakers, calling them each on stage as she read their biographical thumbnails aloud. Before she could wrap up Keir and Posh's self-aggrandizing bio—it was strange for a contestant's intro to include the terms "super fit" and "age-defying"—Lemmy hopped onto the dais and swiped the microphone out of her hand.

As Pauley stood there, paralyzed by his absolute cheek, Lemmy said, "All right, ladies and gentlemen, no more foreplay, it's time for the main event. I'm Lemmy Beaglehole, your humble judge. Separating the wheat from the chaff and the sweet from the daft."

No one laughed. Feet shifted under tables; someone coughed.

Turning to Pauley, Lemmy feigned surprise she was still there. "Oh, dear. Still clinging on to your fifteen minutes, are you? *Psst.* Sweetheart, you're free to go. Oh, don't look so hurt. Isn't she lovely, folks? Round of applause for Ms. Pauley Gwyn. Our own Wednesday Addams, and the last of the St. Morwenna Gwyns!"

Scant applause, mostly from Jem and Hack. As Pauley started to exit the dais, Lemmy turned confidingly to the audience and added, "Can you lot keep a secret? She used to be my girl."

"You—*flapdoodle!*" Aghast, Pauley snatched the microphone back. "First, that was a very long time ago. Second, you may be picking the winner, Lemmy, but that doesn't mean you're in charge. Go sit in the judge's seat. Now. Or I'll put you there."

Scattered chuckles among the audience. Startled by the sound, Pauley smiled out at them, meeting Jem's eyes. The mood had turned. Now these people wanted her to succeed, if only to spite Lemmy.

Pushing a lock of hair behind her ear, she announced with greater surety, "As I've introduced our contestants, it's time to bring out the first of their scrumptious creations. Each dessert will be presented blind, so our judge may evaluate each one for taste and visual appeal without any idea which baker it belongs to."

She wheeled out the trolley, which really did look amazing, and allowed herself to bask in some genuine *oohs* and *ahhs*. "Presented for your consideration, Mr. Beaglehole, entry number one. A double layer chocolate crumb with raspberry filling," she said, placing the entire cake before him. "Shaped like a heart, the universal symbol of love and romance, it's covered with dark chocolate ganache and finished with candied raspberries."

"Yes, well, the name Valentine's Bake Off has been taken quite literally, hasn't it? And if I'm being honest, chocolate and raspberry is a painfully obvious combination. No points for originality. All right, Pauls. Be an angel and slice me a piece. Not too large. Some of us are watching our hips."

That's your idea of wit and you slam Isolde for unoriginality? she thought, hoping Lemmy had already forgotten which dessert went with which contestant. Cutting a perfect wedge, she held it up so everyone could admire its double layers and red raspberry ooze. Lemmy tasted it, making a great show of being unimpressed.

"Now on to entry number two. A royal cherry trifle."
Pauley held up Camille's dessert in the Godinger's Dublin
Crystal, which sparkled under the lights. Consulting her
notes, she read, "It consists of madeira cake cut into slices,
ratafia biscuits broken into pieces, cherry brandy, double
cream—Lord, don't we love double cream?—and cherry
conserves. Plus, some whole cherries for good measure.
Here you are, Lemmy."

Dishing up a generous portion, she placed it before
Lemmy, who sat scowling. He didn't pick up his spoon. The
seconds ticked by.

"Lemmy?"

The judge didn't respond. Why was he scowling? He
seemed to have abandoned his Paul Hollywood persona and
begun channeling Simon Cowell.

"Lem?" Pauley nudged him.

"That first cake was a disgrace. Raspberry sauce must
have turned," he muttered. His words were close enough to
the microphone to carry clearly over the speakers.

"All right, Lemmy, this is still just the tasting phase. So,
let's move on to entry number two," Pauley said with determined brightness.

"That bloody sauce wrecked my palate," Lemmy
complained, voice cracking. "My throat's on fire. I need
water. Get me water."

Pauley looked around helplessly. A few guests were
drinking bottled water, but no one seemed to have an
unopened one to share. Out in the corridor, a tall figure in a
flapping brown coat passed by. Though the man—or woman
—glanced into the ballroom, a pink floppy sun hat
concealed the face.

Beside her, Lemmy shuddered, pushing the plated trifle

away. "How can I eat that? Looks like something the dog sicked up."

"Just taste it, why don't you," someone in the audience called.

"Because my tongue's gone numb," Lemmy cried, looking around wildly as Pauley ventured into the audience to appeal for help. "Water! Where is it?"

Someone, she wasn't sure who, put a bottle in his hand. Clumsily, Lemmy twisted off the lid. He knocked back a great quantity—or tried to. The water came spewing back out.

"Lemmy!" Pauley cried.

The judge tried to answer, but no sounds came. His face was dead white; cords stood out on his neck. In a struggle to rise, he kicked over his chair. Tottering around the table, Lemmy made it halfway to the stairs before a massive spasm shook his entire body. The water bottle fell from his hands. Then he toppled off the stage.

"Poison," someone cried. "Help him, he's been poisoned!"

10

"WHO BAKED THE CAKE?"

"Mad Poisoner! I heard..."

"King Triton's..."

"First the policeman almost died. Now this. A poisoner..."

"... said the culprit was never caught..."

As Jem listened, the buzzing among the guests grew more panicked. It seemed Mrs. Jones's rumor about King Triton's was rapidly cross-pollinating among the Bay View's stranded travelers. Some of the voices sounded almost hysterical.

Near the dais, Pauley was trying to get Lemmy back on his feet, without any luck. Was he fighting her? Jem stood up, but even with her height advantage, she couldn't be sure. Scrambling around tables and chairs, she fought her way to Lemmy from one side, while Hack rushed in from the other. If he wasn't up to another emergency so soon after his own, he gave no sign.

"What's happening?" Fernsby demanded, breathless. He looked as if he'd sprinted all the way from his office.

"He tasted one of the cakes and collapsed. Now he's

convulsing." Pauley looked wildly from Jem to Hack. "What should we do?"

Hack, the nearest thing among them to a qualified first responder, knelt at Lemmy's side, looking like a man who desperately wanted to render aid but had no idea where to start. Fernsby, meanwhile, looked around as if thirsting for a wide column. Finding himself bereft, he drifted over to the judging area, as if on the scent of a crucial clue. Jem watched in amazement as he inspected the table, peeked behind the red curtain, and nimbly disappeared behind it.

When she looked back at Lemmy, she found his thrashing had weakened to the occasional twitch. His eyes were open but glassy, fixed on nothing. Except for her, Hack, Pauley, and Micki, everyone else kept their distance. Some stared. Most averted their eyes.

"Is he breathing?" she asked Pauley.

"I don't think so."

"Need my kit," Hack muttered, patting himself down. "Penlight. Penlight. Anyone got a penlight?"

Jem turned on her mobile's torch and passed it over. Hack monkeyed around with shining the light in Lemmy's unblinking eyes, then asked, "Who has a mirror?"

"I do," said Trevor's grandmother, Mrs. Morton. She dug in her bag, hand-crocheted to match her wrap, and came up with a round compact. Hack put it in front of Lemmy's mouth and nostrils, but it revealed no respiration.

Sighing, Hack took out his penknife, extended the blade, and pressed the point under two of Lemmy's fingernails. Jem and the onlookers shuddered, but Lemmy seemed beyond pain.

"Right. I'm calling it. He's dead." Hack stood up. "Fernsby!" he shouted at the man behind the curtain.

"Come out and secure the exit. No one is leaving this room until I say. No one."

Sheepishly, Fernsby emerged from behind the curtain. Looking unhappy, he took a deep breath and strode to block the exit just before Sebastian A. Minting and family attempted to pass through.

"I'm sorry, Mr. Minting, but you heard Sergeant Hackman. No one can leave. Surely you understand," he pleaded as the imperious guest stared him down. "It's only temporary. An unavoidable inconvenience."

"Inconvenience? You've already made me a paying guest against my will. That was an inconvenience. This is rank cruelty. Look at my wife. She's on the verge of being physically ill. To keep us here until you say otherwise is unconscionable."

"More like uncomfortable. But necessary," Hack said. When the man whirled to confront him, Hack smiled unpleasantly.

"Mr. Minting, we've been jousting for a while, but now I want you to listen to me very carefully. If you put one foot into the corridor, I'll arrest you."

"For what, precisely?"

"Obstruction of justice. You just witnessed a sudden death. Possibly by misadventure, but more likely by murder. We all did," he said, glancing around the ballroom to include everyone in his warning. "Odds are, someone in this room is responsible for Beaglehole's death. Or if not responsible," he amended, his gaze sliding from face to face, "capable of giving evidence which will help the killer to be caught and punished. Which you have a legal and moral obligation to do. Therefore, no one is leaving until they've been questioned to my satisfaction."

"When a little man gets a scintilla of power, the results

are ugly to behold," Minting told Hack. "I'm not afraid of you. Moreover, I won't subject my family to the sight of that man's corpse a moment longer. We'll be in suite 108. Question us there, or not at all."

The man looked serious, damn him. Afraid that Hack might not be physically up to a confrontation with Minting after his own crisis that morning, Jem rushed to chime in. "Mr. Minting, I don't blame you for wanting to get your family away from the sight of... Pauls! Can you cover Lemmy with something?"

"Sure. I mean..." She turned and yanked a white linen cloth off the nearest table, accidentally managing to leave the electric votive and posy magically in place. Mrs. Morton gave her light applause. Pauley, looking mortified by her impromptu trick, hurriedly draped the tablecloth over Lemmy's corpse.

"Right. Sorted." Jem looked Minting in the eye. "Please, Mr. Minting. People look up to you. Think of the example you're setting. If you and your family flout the rules, everyone else will try to do the same. Evidence could be moved or destroyed. If there's a conspiracy, stories could be hatched for mutual exoneration. Hack has no mainland support. He has to control the scene and question witnesses while their memories are not only fresh, but unadulterated."

She didn't expect anything from Minting but more bile. He was one of those beady-eyed, superior types who seemed to believe he could out-stare a King cobra. A human mongoose, he was up on his back legs, bristling with a show of ferocity, trying to seem bigger than he really was.

What is he so afraid of? she wondered.

"Darling," Minting's wife murmured, touching his arm. "She's right."

"Dad, please," said one of his sons. It was the older,

taller one, who'd previously been sitting with his eyes closed. Now, like his mum, he looked rather nauseous, as if on the brink of vomiting. "Let's sit down and do as she asks."

"It's not like there's anything to do in the suite," the younger son said. "Even the ruddy telly's out."

"May I remind you there are such things as books?" Minting shot back. The boy, perhaps seventeen, looked away. Though he was much too old for it, he seemed on the verge of tears. His elder brother placed a comforting hand on his shoulder.

"Mr. Minting, I give you my word." Hack deployed a smooth, conciliatory tone that came from years of working with the public. "I will question everyone politely and with dispatch. If in our previous conversation I came across before as overbearing or disrespectful, I apologize. And if you and your family will set an example for the rest of the guests, I'd be beyond grateful."

Damn, he's good, Jem thought, watching Minting's face relax as he visibly decided to stand down. He led his family back to their table. They all sat down, the younger son still looking gutted, the mum seeming steadier, and the elder boy still slightly green.

"All right, everyone," Hack told the room at large. "First, I'll go from table to table and take down names and identifying information. Once I have a list of everyone present, I'll split you into groups and go from there. Jem, you're with me."

Jem goggled at him but didn't have to be asked twice. As she zipped to his side, one of the guests asked archly, "Is the lovely civilian suddenly a deputy?"

"Under the circumstances, I'd say yes. Yes, she is." He looked at Jem. "You don't mind officially helping with my investigation, do you?"

"I thought you'd never ask."

To make the lists, Fernsby produced some Bay View branded pens and notepads. With those in hand, Jem and Hack made rounds among the audience, collecting four data points from each witness: name, date of birth, home mailing address, and room number.

After all the audience members were properly identified, Hack issued a blanket invitation: anyone who believed they might possess helpful information was welcome to step into the corridor and tell him privately. Jem looked around hopefully, but there were no takers.

Three possibilities for why. They genuinely didn't see anything, they did see something but failed to register its importance, or they're in on the murder.

She scanned the onlookers surreptitiously, searching for odd affects or suspicious behavior, but perceived nothing out of the ordinary. People seemed frightened, shocked, angry, annoyed. It all seemed about standard, apart from Minting's weepy younger son, who occasionally swiped at his eyes.

"All right," Hack told the guests. "Now I'm going to turn my attention to the contestants, anyone connected to the Bake Off, and the hotel staff. That means I'd like the rest of you to give us the room, please."

Instant relieved chatter rose among the thwarted travelers. The words "Decant Resist" were heard several times.

"Now I realize this won't be popular, but I'd like everyone to stay in their own rooms. I know, it seems like an arbitrary demand," he added when guests immediately began to grumble. "But I remind you, there's been a murder. Given the weather, it's quite likely the killer is among us in the hotel. So, while I don't want you unduly alarmed, I also don't want you roaming about, potentially putting yourselves in danger."

"I'll ring Xavier on the house phone," Fernsby piped up suddenly. "He'll be pleased to serve drinks as takeaway, so to speak, if you'll forgive the indignity of paper cups."

That did the trick. Out filed the guests, including the Minting family, and if they didn't look pleased with their situation, they seemed keen on a spot of wine or liquor to go.

"I have no idea how many people the hotel employs, or which ones are salient to this investigation," Hack murmured near Jem's ear. "Let's focus on the bakers first."

This next class of suspects silently occupied two adjacent tables. Mrs. Jones, Mrs. Morton, Trevor, Isolde, and Camille sat at one table; Keir, Posh, Pauley, Micki, and Fernsby at the other. Hack positioned himself in front of the dais so he could observe all of them at once, but to Jem's eyes he was already sagging. Without asking his permission, she picked up a stray chair and placed it in front of him with a thump, so he had no choice but to take a load off. That accomplished, she stepped behind him, pen and paper in hand, to assist with both observation and notetaking. It was nice to be invited into the investigation, as opposed to insinuating herself through the cracks.

"Now. Contestants. It's not that I want you to feel like you're on the spot," Hack said, in that monotone copper voice which made it clear they were, in fact, on the spot. "But I'm afraid I must ask, who baked the cake that made Lemmy sick? Heart-shaped chocolate with raspberry filling?"

Isolde had lost her Miss Piggy-esque defiance. In fact, she was turning a lighter shade of Kermit. Opening her mouth to answer, she suddenly vomited all over the tablecloth.

Mrs. Morton pushed her chair back.

"Oh, you poor love," Mrs. Jones cried.

Camille yelped. "Wow! Incoming. Admission of guilt."

"She's not guilty. She's scared," said a man in a powerful voice. Jem was puzzled. It seemed to emanate from Trevor's lips. Was there a ventriloquist?

Apparently not. Suiting action to words, Trevor bundled up the tablecloth and strode across the room, stuffing it into the rubbish bin. Though a sour odor hung in the air, the offending sight was gone. That accomplished, he resumed his seat next to Isolde and regarded everyone else watchfully, like her faithful dog.

As Mrs. Jones rummaged through her bag, Mrs. Morton asked, "Do you want tissues, Lobelia?"

"No, I have a travel pack." Mrs. Jones handed it to her granddaughter. "Isolde's always had a weak tum."

Weeping brokenly, Isolde dabbed her eyes with a wad of tissue. Trevor watched her, looking desperate to help but unable to think how.

"Muh-muh-muh bakery," she wailed. "It was my cake. From muh-muh bakery. And now Lemmy Beaglehole is dead."

"Yes, well. Silver linings, like I always say." Mrs. Jones patted her granddaughter's arm. "But don't assume the worst of Sergeant Hackman. Someone poisoned him just this morning, and it couldn't possibly have been you. Furthermore, you haven't been in custody of your cake every moment. Someone must have doctored it after you turned it over to Pauley."

"I don't know if that's possible," Pauley began, but Hack halted her by lifting his palm.

"First things first," he said. "Isolde, tell me about the cake. When did you actually bake it?"

"First thing this morning."

"Was anyone present with you?"

"No."

"Throughout the entire process, it was just you and the cake? No customers to interrupt?"

"I decided not to open today on account of the Bake Off. No one in their right mind would buy from me on the day free samples are given out, after the contest."

Jem said, "The icing was pretty elaborate. Did you do it before or after you rushed over here to get your gran off the floor?"

"Before." Isolde dabbed at her eyes again.

Jem waited for Hack to remind Isolde about what she'd said before several witnesses—that the news about her grandmother had possibly led her to accidentally leave Cake Me Proud's door unlocked. But Hack was wheezing faintly. When he did speak, he only muttered, "I don't suppose anyone has a water to spare?"

She glanced meaningfully at Pauley, who hopped up, saying, "I'll snag you a sealed bottle from somewhere, Hack." Judging by the bakers' faces, everyone was reaching the same unfortunate conclusion; Hack was still far less than a hundred percent after his brush with death.

"Isolde," Jem said. "I seem to remember you said something about rushing back because you might have forgotten to lock up. Did you?"

"Yes," Isolde said eagerly. "I'll swear to it. I'll swear right this minute."

"That won't be necessary," Hack said, opening the water Pauley gave him and taking a grateful swig. "Do you mean to say you left the shop door unlocked, or your home door?"

"The bakery. But it's connected to our place inside, and the pass-through door is always open. So, both."

"You reside with your gran, Mrs. Jones?" Hack asked.

"Yes."

"Anyone else?"

"No."

"Do you have employees or friends who are permitted to enter and exit as they please?"

"No, I'm a one-woman operation." She gave a bitter laugh. "Or I was."

"It'll be all right," Trevor murmured. He sounded like himself again—diffident, like a sullen teen—but Jem thought his effort to console his ex-wife was sincere. "Even if you lose the bakery, it's not the end of the world."

Isolde continued dabbing her eyes as if he hadn't spoken, but Mrs. Morton and Mrs. Jones took notice. Both gaped at Trevor as if they couldn't believe their ears.

"Well, it's not," he whispered, looking away.

"Right, so the place was unlocked," Hack said. "But you have no reason to believe any particular person might have been around the cake while you were away, is that right? Good. Now, did you visually inspect the cake when you—"

"Just a moment, Hack," Jem interrupted apologetically. "Isolde, has anyone been sleeping rough in the area or panhandling around your shop?"

She looked nonplussed. "The weather's still too uncertain for rough sleeping. And a panhandler's liable to get told off about things being tough all over, in the off-season."

So much for the person I glimpsed ducking into the stairwell. It was a longshot, anyway.

Isolde continued, "And yes, Sergeant Hackman, I looked my cake over before I boxed it up. It was perfect."

"Did you seal the box?"

"Yes."

Hack looked at Pauley. "Can you verify that it was sealed when you received it?"

"Yes."

"Right. Back to the cake's creation. During the baking process, did you taste the batter? The filling? Any part of it?"

"Of course not. I'm a professional baker." Isolde sounded affronted. "I don't lick my fingers or the spoon. I always wear gloves and adhere to the highest health and safety standards. My last inspection score was one hundred percent."

"All right," Hack said mildly. He was wheezing louder now. "About what time did you surrender your cake to Ms. Gwyn?"

"About ten minutes before the Bake Off started."

"Closer to thirty," Pauley said. "There were some delays, remember?"

"Were the cakes in your possession from that moment on?"

"Yes. Wait. I mean, technically, yes, but they weren't always in my sight," Pauley said. "They were on a trolley behind the red curtain. I left it back there when I realized Micki hadn't turned in Clarence's bio. We put our heads together to create one. So, the trolley was out of my sight for a few minutes."

"How many?" Hack coughed weakly. "Minutes, I mean."

"I don't know. Five. Ten," Pauley said. "Then I asked

where Lemmy was, and someone said he was behind the curtain."

"That was me," Camille announced proudly. "I'm detail oriented. Always noticing things. And if I'm being honest, I'm a bit of a Scilly Sleuth myself. Currently working on the Crab Pots Caper."

No one replied to that. Micki, however, gave Camille a sidelong glance.

"You saw Lemmy go behind the curtain?" Hack asked, stifling another cough.

"Yes. The moment Pauley and Micki put their heads together, he was on the move. So, he was probably alone with the cakes for close to ten minutes." Her eyes widened. "Here's a brainwave. What if he poisoned himself?"

This time she got the side-eye from every direction. Ignoring that, Hack asked Pauley, "Then you confronted him?"

"Of course. Not that that had any effect. I asked Lemmy if he'd read my notes, which would tell him who baked which unboxed dessert. He said, 'Maybe.' Then he showed me the icing on his fingers and said he'd sampled the goods."

Groans and looks of disgust passed among the bakers.

"I know," Pauley said rather defensively. "But the show must go on. And I switched the order of the cakes to throw him off. Isolde's wasn't meant to go first, but it did."

Hack tried to ask a follow-up, but a stronger wave of coughing seized him. After more water, he said hoarsely, "So, Pauley, if I understand you correctly, the only two people with access to Isolde's cake after she handed it over was you and Lemmy."

"Not exactly." Rising, Pauley crossed to the red curtain and pushed it aside. This revealed the ballroom's rear portion, previously hidden from all the contestants.

"Where does that door lead to?" Micki asked.

"It's not marked," Pauley said. "I didn't even notice it earlier when I was putting up decorations. But when I started loading cakes on the trolley, I saw it was ajar. So maybe someone came or went that way."

"Sergeant Hackman." Minting re-entered Ballroom A, followed by his eldest son. "I'm sorry to interrupt, but I thought you should know. There seems to be a trespasser inside the hotel."

11

"LES POISSONS"

"A trespasser? What does he look like?" Jem asked. She should've allowed Hack to ask the first question, of course, but he was once again drinking water to stave off another coughing fit.

Minting said, "I only saw him for a moment. As we returned to our suite, my son, Jace, noticed a man trying door handles in the corridor. Jace tried to talk to him, but the man took off walking. When I called out sharply, he broke into a run. Literally ran away, like a criminal."

"But what did he look like? Skin tone? Hair?"

"No idea," said Jace Minting. "But he wore a hoodie. And he was on the short side."

"Brown coat?"

"No, just a hoodie."

"Pink floppy hat?" Pauley asked.

As Jace shook his head, Jem turned to her friend. "So, you saw him, too?"

"Just for a second. He passed through the corridor just outside the ballroom."

"When?"

"Around the time Lemmy got sick."

Hack, again fighting a cough, managed to ask, "Minting. When the man in the hoodie ran... where did he..."

"Into a stairwell. Sergeant Hackman." Minting looked down his nose at him imperiously. "You don't look well, man. Are you quite sure you're capable of conducting this invest—"

"Let me take a look," Jace broke in, stepping forward. "Sergeant Hackman, it looks as if you're breaking out again. Don't worry, it's only mild hives at the moment. I understand you experienced anaphylactic shock earlier today. Has anything like this ever happened to you before?"

Hack shook his head. "Not until I drank the lemon water," he said with effort.

"Do you reckon there's an airborne toxin?" Camille asked, apparently determined to offer her keen insights on every angle of the situation. "A new virus, maybe? Or a carbon monoxide leak?"

The contestants looked around anxiously.

"Absolutely not," Jace announced with unexpected authority. "Don't panic. I can assure you this isn't carbon monoxide poisoning or anything contagious. Sergeant Hackman appears to be suffering from what's known as biphasic anaphylaxis. Secondary anaphylaxis, if you will."

As Jem and the others goggled at Jace, his father said, "My son will attend Oxford Medical School in the autumn. He's completed his pre-med studies and done a bit of volunteer work, shadowing doctors at the local clinic. But I must remind him, he's not a qualified physician."

"That's right. Still, I can make an educated guess." Jace gave Hack's shoulder a friendly pat. "I know this must feel a bit alarming, but secondary anaphylaxis isn't uncommon. Think of it as a physiological aftershock. Your body dealt with the inciting event, but there are still ripples in the pond, slowly evening themselves out."

"As far as I know, there was only one adrenaline pen in the hotel," Jem said. "Will Hack be okay without another dose?"

"Yes. His breathing already sounds better. He's come through the worst. This will be nothing by comparison." The young man smiled at Hack, who smiled back.

Awesome bedside manner, kiddo, Jem thought admiringly. *You may not be qualified yet, but you've already nailed the reassurance part.*

Jace continued. "When this is over, if you're still experiencing symptoms, your GP may choose to prescribe a course of oral steroids. But for now, rest and fluids are your best bet."

"There's been a murder," Hack said. "I can't rest. Turns out the crime scene has another access point." Rising unsteadily, he pointed to the open door at the ballroom's rear. "I need to check it—"

"No, you don't," Jem said, pushing him back into the chair. "I'll go and report back."

"Right. I'll go with you," Camille announced, popping up like a jack-in-the-box.

"No, you won't. You're a suspect," Jem said with satisfaction.

"I'll go," Micki said.

"Technically also a suspect. If I'm being fair," Jem said, cringing slightly at her friend's expression.

"Surely that doesn't apply to me," Pauley said, half-rising.

"Oh, yes it does," Micki said, yanking her back down.

"I'll go," Fernsby said reluctantly.

"No. You stay with me," Hack said.

Fernsby and the others looked surprised, but Jem understood Hack's reasoning, if no one else did. In his weakened
state, he didn't want to risk being alone with the murder's
prime suspects. They looked like a harmless bunch—two
septuagenarians, mopey Trevor, weepy Isolde, little Keir,
Material Middle-Aged Girl Posh, and Camille, who seemed
more of a talker than a fighter. But Jem had learned not to
be fooled by surface impressions. One of the most ruthless
killers she'd ever met had initially struck her as a shy
schoolboy.

"I'll go with you," Sebastian Minting announced.

Hack blinked at him. So did Jem, who briefly wondered
if he were being sarcastic.

"Well, why not? Didn't you lecture me on doing my bit,
Ms. Jago?"

"Um. Right. Let's do it," she said, briefly wondering
how he'd picked up her name. She'd heard him tell Hack he
was from Exeter? As the Scilly Sleuth, she'd garnered a bit
of tabloid attention, but not from the sort of publications a
man like Minting seemed likely to peruse.

"Remember," Hack said hoarsely as they set off to
examine the open door and what looked like a room beyond.
"Touch nothing with your fingers if you can avoid it. Not
even a light switch."

The open door led to a small culinary staging room.
Using their mobile torches to pierce the gloom, Jem and
Minting found it spotless and tidy, as if it hadn't been used
lately. The two sinks were dry, the warming trays were
stacked ten high, and the shelves held buffet items: chafing
dishes, canned heat, empty champagne buckets.

For formal gatherings, Jem thought. *This is how the staff
keeps the nibbles warm.*

At the rear of the staging room was another door. Not

wanting to touch the knob and possibly muddle any finger-prints, Jem looked about for a napkin or towel.

"Here." Minting offered an old-fashioned linen hand-kerchief. It was embroidered with his initials, *sMa*.

"Oh. Cheers." Turning the knob with the handkerchief, Jem opened the door. Instantly her senses were assaulted with music, light, and odor.

The music was loud and pleasant—a dance club number with a heavy beat and few words. The light, fluorescent, was garish and inescapable. As for the odors, they were legion; coffee, onions, vinegar, and bleach. It was the kitchen of Kestrel & Peregrine, Bay View's two-rosette-award-winning restaurant.

Hard at work was a staff of about ten, each person uniformed in white and laboring at their individual stations. In the center of the kitchen, a redhead in a tall white toque was whispering with a subordinate.

It took a few seconds for Jem and Minting's presence to be noted. Finally, a cook looked up, saw them, and switched off the music. The woman in the toque broke off her whispered conversation, staring at them in apparent disbelief.

"This is... what?" she asked in a thick French accent. Her colleague, a pear-shaped young man whose curly brown hair was covered with a food service hairnet, gave Jem and Minting a deer-in-the-headlights look.

"I'm sorry to interrupt your work," Jem said. "I know you were playing music in here. But are you actually unaware of what happened in Ballroom A a few minutes ago?"

The woman turned to her colleague. "Am I being troubled with hotel nonsense?"

"The kitchen has nothing to do with venue issues," said the young man, who still looked frightened by Jem and

Minting's sudden appearance. "You'll want Mr. Fernsby, out front."

"A man is dead," Minting snapped, going for the jugular. "He ate poisoned food."

"*Sacre bleu!*" the white-coated woman cried. This was followed by more French, all machine-gun rapid, all obscene. Jem's French was like her Italian—shameful—but she recognized most of the curse words. This chef subscribed to the Gordon Ramsay school of emotional regulation.

"I never said it was your food," Minting corrected. "No need to get hysterical."

Jem cringed inside. Judging by the woman's expression, she took that loaded word as an insult. And judging by the collection of knives stuck to a wall-mounted magnetic strip, she knew at least fifty ways to peel flesh off the bone.

"Let's start over," she said diplomatically. "I'm Jem Jago. This is Sebastian Minting. The judge of the Bake Off, Lemmy Beaglehole, died while tasting one of the cakes. We're working off the hypothesis it may have been tampered with before the contest started. There was access to the cakes at the rear of the ballroom. And since the door to the staging room was open, we checked it out, and it led us here."

"You are police?"

"No, but Sergeant Hackman is here, and he empowered us to help him. No one can call in reinforcements from the mainland until the storm breaks. Now may I ask, who are you?"

"Chef de cuisine," the woman said coldly. "You just admitted this accident has nothing to do with the kitchen. Please do tell me why you are here, interrupting my work and asking me improper questions." As she spoke, her

French accent somehow became even more French. Often, she infused her words with a strangled honk—a *hon-hon-hon*. It reminded Jem of the chef in Disney's *The Little Mermaid*, who chased Sebastian the crab around his kitchen with a butcher's knife while singing the immortal, "Les Poissons."

"Well, it's obvious, isn't it?" Minting said. "There's easy access from the kitchen to the ballroom. Someone tampered with the cake. Why couldn't it be one of you lot?"

"Outrageous. Has anyone stepped out of this kitchen in the last two hours?" the chef de cuisine demanded.

"No, Chef," the white coats shouted in unison.

"There. Now go away."

"I really think you owe us more than that," Jem said. "Something's going on here. Did you hear what happened to Sergeant Hackman earlier? Water from the glass decanter in the lobby made his throat close up. He could have died."

The chef de cuisine responded with that most French of all gestures, the one-shouldered shrug.

"There's no medical support to be had out here. None," Minting said with sudden passion. "If you value your own health, you should help us figure out what happened, not obstruct us."

Jem studied him surreptitiously, intrigued. When Minting abruptly offered to assist her, it had crossed her mind that the easiest way for a guilty person to hide in plain sight was to glom on to the investigation. Especially with an amateur like herself, who might presumably be easier to fool than a seasoned pro like Hack. But unless her deductive skills had completely atrophied, Minting was sincere. His distress was as real now as it had been earlier, when he'd realized they were well and truly cut off until the storm ended.

"Fine," the chef de cuisine said at last. "But I must attend my sauces. Do not bother me. Bother Gregory." She drifted away to the far side of the room, where a cooker covered with steel pots sat between the walk-in freezer and the door marked, SCULLERY.

"I'm Gregory Howard. *Boulanger*," said the man in the hairnet. Pointing to the rest of the staff, he identified each by name and rank: *plongeur, poissonnier, commis* chef to the *poissonnier, saucier,* and *friturier.*

"Pleased to meet you all." Jem aimed a smile at each of the cooks, though few looked her way. They all seemed to be intent on their various duties—mixing, chopping, stirring —yet the general tension was still palpable. "Now about the Bake Off. Did anyone in here help out with the Ballroom preparations? Even in a small way?"

"I didn't even know it was happening," Gregory said. "Sometimes the kitchen staff is asked to cater an event. Otherwise, we stick to our regular duties."

"Okay. I don't want to belabor the point, but I have to ask: did you enter Ballroom A in the last hour?"

"No."

"What about your boss? Or anyone working in this room?"

"No."

"We are quite busy preparing for dinner, as anyone looking can see," called the chef de cuisine from her place overlooking the sauces.

"A dinner no one will dare eat. I shouldn't waste my time if I were you," Minting shot back.

"Anyone who considers my kitchen unsafe is cordially invited to starve."

"There's also been talk of trespassers inside the hotel," Jem said, still hoping to catch the eye of someone less prickly and more inclined to talk. "One was a shorter man wearing a hoodie. The other was a tall man or woman in a brown coat and pink hat."

"That's odd," Gregory said. "Pink hat? Really?"

"Have you seen anyone matching those descriptions?"

"We have seen strangers in this hotel every day of our lives," the chef de cuisine said.

"I see several possible hiding places," Minting announced, getting his back up again. "What's that?"

"Walk-in freezer. Too cold for anyone to linger," Gregory said with a nervous laugh.

"And that room?" Minting pointed.

"The scullery. But, er, no one's in there at the moment. The dishwashers are taking a break." Gregory offered a weak smile.

"Can you pass through the scullery into another part of the hotel?" Jem asked.

"This is ridiculous," the chef de cuisine exploded. "Allow me to prove to you that we are not harboring cake-poisoners."

She rapped theatrically on the scullery door. Then, opening it a few inches, she slipped inside. Though she closed it behind her, she shouted loud enough to be heard clearly in the kitchen proper, "Is any bad person hiding in here?"

Opening the door from inside the scullery, the chef de cuisine held it wide so Jem and Minting could see inside. The room was unlit, the conveyor belt slumbering between the huge industrial machines that washed and dried the dishes. "As you see. No murderers."

"I see a door," Minting said. "Where does it lead?"

"To the cloakroom. And beyond that is the courtyard, and the dormitories where we sleep. You're welcome to look there, too, if you don't mind being blown away. Au revoir!" Returning to Gregory's side, she stage-whispered, "Get them out. Now."

"We'll go," Jem said, deciding there was nothing more to be gained from antagonizing her further. "But we may be back with Sergeant Hackman soon. And be warned—the storm may have driven some people into the hotel in search of shelter. They might be harmless. Down on their luck. Or they might be homicidal maniacs. Who can say?"

"Cheers," Minting added caustically, and Jem had the satisfaction of seeing the chef de cuisine rendered momentarily speechless.

Re-entering Ballroom A, Jem expected to find Hack in the midst of systematically interviewing the contestants. But Hack wasn't there. Neither was Micki.

The tables were empty. The contestants had withdrawn to the furthest corner of the room and seemed to be in a huddle—the worst possible activity for suspects whose alibis had not yet been etched in stone. Meanwhile, Pauley sat on the floor beside Jace Minting, who looked pale and ill.

12

CIRCULAR FIRING SQUAD

"Jace," Minting cried, sprinting to his son's side as Jem demanded of Pauley, "Where's Hack?"

"Up in our room. He's fine, Jemmie. Micki's with him, just in case. He needs a rest. And Jace here has an upset tum," Pauley explained. "Better now that he's got it all out."

"Sorry, Dad." Jace smiled at his father. "It was the smell from that bin. You know me. When someone sicks up, I sick up, too. Never mind all that. Any luck? Did you two detect anything worthwhile?"

"No," Minting said. "I should have stayed with you."

"I think you were helpful. A natural bad cop," Jem said truthfully. "The facts are still being collected. But what we learned could prove helpful."

"I'm getting you back to the suite," Minting told Jace. "Sergeant Hackman isn't the only one who needs a lie down."

"That's not on, I'm afraid," Jace said. "You know Mum and Nigel. They'll see I've been poorly, and they'll crowd me, and I'll feel worse from sheer aggravation. It's a feed-back loop. Why don't we go to the library instead? No one's ever in there. I'll look at that book of vintage cars until I'm steady again."

"All right." Minting looked around. "Where's Fernsby?"

"Agnetha came to fetch him," Pauley said. "Someone else complained about seeing a tramp in the hall. The one in the coat and hat."

Jem groaned. "We really need to track him down. I'll say this, if he's a killer, he has the world's most eye-catching disguise."

"Do you really think someone broke in here to poison a cake?" Minting asked Jem. He didn't sound sarcastic. He sounded baffled. And he seemed to genuinely want her opinion.

"I think it's more likely he just took refuge out of the storm. But stranger things have happened. Go on. Take your son to the library." Seeing the uncertainty in his eyes, she added, "If Hack is down for the count and I need backup, I'll call on you and Fernsby, I promise. But first I need to question those bakers. C'mon, Pauley."

"Feel better, Jace," Pauley called to the Mintings as they departed. To Jem she added in a whisper, "Something's really wrong there."

"So I gathered. Could it be cancer?"

"Lord, I hope not. And he doesn't look like he's doing chemo. Maybe the family's just overprotective. But I wouldn't bet on it."

They approached the bakers' huddle, but no one acknowledged them. Jem was about to clap her hands and ask for attention, but Pauley put two fingers in her mouth and let out an ear-piercing whistle. Everyone jumped.

"Right. Here's our situation, lovelies," Pauley announced, as if still Mistress of Ceremonies. "Sergeant Hackman will recover from whatever he ingested, but in the meantime, we have a corpse on the floor and no one but Isolde has answered any questions. It's time for Jem to interview the rest of you."

The contestants appeared dubious. Mrs. Jones was the first to speak. "Well, why not? She *is* the Scilly Sleuth."

"I read about her in *Bright Star*," Mrs. Morton added. "They positively delight in posting the most unflattering pictures, don't they? But the story was quite positive."

"I'll answer more questions," Isolde said dully. "I have nothing to hide." She gestured to her ex-husband. "C'mon, Trev."

As the four of them returned to their table, Keir and Posh swapped glances. Keir said, "We'll stay because we also don't have anything to hide. But we reserve the right not to answer your questions. You aren't a trained investigator, and you don't have the authority." They returned to the adjacent table, followed by Camille.

"I'll answer your questions. One sleuth should help another," she told Jem in what was probably meant to be an ingratiating tone. "But don't you think we should secure the evidence first?"

"The desserts? Oh, of course, yes, I was just about to say that," Jem lied, embarrassed by her lapse. "After we talk, you can each return your entry to its proper container. We'll find some tape and reseal the boxes."

"Then what? We can't leave them sitting out for hours," Camille said. "It might degrade the samples. Forensically," she added, clearly enjoying the feel of that word in her mouth. "I'll bet the hotel kitchen has one of those walk-in freezers. We can store the cakes in there."

"I don't care for the sound of that," Keir said.

Mrs. Jones sighed.

"What? I'm only looking out for myself and Posh," he

said. "Once our entries are out of our control, anything might happen to them. There's no crime scene tape. No detectives guarding the integrity of the investigation. Suppose little Miss Marple here decides she wants to be featured in *Bright Star* again? She could dose all our cakes with ricin and call this *Murder on the Orient Express*."

"That was Poirot, not Marple," said Mrs. Morton, drumming her fingers on the tabletop.

"Gran, stop. You're making me nervous," said Trevor. What had he said to his ex-wife during the huddle? Now that they were seated again, he kept trying to make eye contact with Isolde, without result.

"I haven't anything to do with my hands," Mrs. Morton complained. "I wish I hadn't forgotten my work bag."

"Not like you to ever be without a crochet needle and yarn," Mrs. Jones said.

"I for one don't think it's fair to suspect Jem Jago of nefarious motives," Camille said. "And it wouldn't be ricin, anyway. Ricin kills very slowly, so it's not a good choice. Plus, it's difficult to obtain."

"Why do you know so much about ricin?" Keir asked.

"It's always the outsiders," murmured Posh.

"Beg pardon?" Camille stared at her.

"I'm only stating a fact. I read that story about Jem Jago, too. When she catches a killer, it's usually a community outsider."

"How can you call me an outsider? I've lived in the islands for three years."

"I've lived in the islands for ten," Posh sniffed. "What do we really know about you, Camille? Other than you like the color pink and you're an authority on deadly poisons?"

"This is getting silly," Pauley said. "Plenty of people know ricin isn't very likely."

"I know," said Mrs. Jones.

"So do I. It was on *Breaking Bad*," Mrs. Morton said primly.

"Your objection is ridiculous," Camille told Keir. "Look at Isolde. She's the prime suspect, and she hasn't made a peep."

Isolde's eyes opened wide. "I'm not the prime suspect. I'm the victim."

"Lemmy's the victim," Keir said.

"Well, I'm the other victim."

"That's right. She's not the prime suspect. You take that back." Trevor demanded of Camille, sounding like Isolde's Year Eight boyfriend.

"Oh, don't go to pieces. I'm only stating a fact," Camille said. "Isolde might even be right. If Lemmy wasn't the target, maybe Isolde was. What better way to ruin a baker?"

"Exactly. I submitted a perfectly lovely cake, and someone used it to commit murder. They're stitching me up," she cried, working herself up into Miss Piggy karate chop territory. "I won't take the fall for this. I won't!"

"You won't have to." Trevor tried putting his arm around Isolde, but she shook him off. "This is all a misunderstanding. When the crime techs get here, they'll find a way to clear your name. They always do."

"On telly, you mean," Posh said.

"Let's follow this possibility," Jem said quickly, determined to get in a question before Ms. Crab Pots Caper took the wheel again. "Isolde, can you think of anyone who might want to hurt you? To shut down Cake Me Proud?"

"Trevor Morton. Isn't it obvious?" Keir burst out. "That woman broke his heart."

"Beat it and creamed it," Posh put in.

Heads swiveled to look at her.

"Beat it and creamed it. You know? Like cake batter?"

"Trevor, do you have anything to say about that?" Jem asked.

"I'd never hurt Isolde," he declared, again trying to make eye contact. His ex-wife folded her arms across her chest and sighed.

"Of course you wouldn't hurt a fly, dear." Mrs. Morton, usually mild, fixed her eyes on Keir. "Why don't you work on your own marriage?"

"What do you mean by that?" Keir looked shocked. Posh put a comforting hand on his arm, but he shook her off.

"I think you know," Mrs. Jones said. "As for Trevor and Isolde, they had an amicable split. Isn't that right, darling?"

"I think the world of Trev," Isolde quavered.

"For the record," Posh announced to the room at large, "Keir and I have a wonderful marriage. We're life partners. We do everything together."

"The better to keep an eye on him," Mrs. Jones said.

"What are you on about, you bitter old bird?" Keir's chest puffed out. "I'm a model husband. I've been devoted to Portia for twenty-two years."

"Yes, but how many times have you gambled away the family silver?" Mrs. Morton asked. To Mrs. Jones, she said, "Remember that sports coupe he used to drive around Hugh Town?"

"Yes. And the bungalow on Tresco. People still talk about how he bungled the bungalow."

Mrs. Morton chuckled. "Then there was his yacht. Sold at a loss to Jimmy Franks's All Marine. Pity about online gaming. Mind you, I used to fancy a bit of a flutter myself."

"But you never lost a home playing blackjack on a computer," Mrs. Jones said, smiling pitilessly at Keir, who was turning red.

"Stop! This is turning into a circular firing squad," Pauley said, appalled.

Jem stifled a groan. Apparently, her junior partner in amateur sleuthing had forgotten the first rule of snooping: *when your suspects start airing one another's dirty laundry, let them.* It wasn't that Pauley didn't want to hear all the possible motives. It was just that something in her Gwyn DNA made her want to keep Scillonians from harming themselves.

"Let's get back on track," Jem said. "Please. You all must see the sense of preserving the cakes by putting them in the walk-in freezer. It might even work in Isolde's favor. As Camille said," she added, forcing herself to throw the eager would-be sleuth a bone, "we want to preserve all forensic traces. Besides, I'm guessing some of you don't have rooms, right?"

"We're in 206," Mrs. Jones reminded her.

"I couldn't get one," Camille said.

"Neither could we," Posh admitted. "But the manager promised us a cot and blanket."

"Right. So, do you want to sign up for guarding your cake all night? It won't make for a very comfortable time in the lobby, sleeping with one eye open while you guard your cake from ricin or whatever," Jem said, trying not to sound as contemptuous as she felt. Something about Keir rubbed her the wrong way.

"I'm freezing my cake," Camille said.

"You'd better believe I am," Isolde said.

"Me, too," Trevor said.

"Of course, I'll do as you ask," Mrs. Morton told Jem warmly.

Keir, who seemed to feel as if these cheerful assents were designed purely to humiliate him, rounded on Jem.

He barely came up to her shoulder, but to his credit, that didn't deter him.

"You think you're the great detective? Fine. Those two mad bats are the guilty parties, mark my words. She"—he pointed a finger at Mrs. Morton—"is a widow whose husband famously died to get away from her. Look how she's raised her grandson to be an emotional cripple. Get your hair out of your face, lad. You're past forty."

"As for you," he continued, looking at Mrs. Jones. "Do you think anyone's forgotten about you lying down in the lobby? You've been on a one-woman crusade against Lemmy ever since he was announced as judge. We all heard you call his death a silver lining. You've always been as monomaniacal and cutthroat as they come. Tell me you wouldn't kill to get your way."

"I'll admit I had a bit of fun with my protest," Mrs. Jones said calmly. "He had no business judging this event. He destroyed Trevor's business, and he reveled in it. But he also harmed Jem's other friend, the one upstairs with Sergeant Hackman. He ruined her singing career. He was no friend to Camille, either, isn't that right, dear? I remember when you used to write for *All Things Penzance*. Then he took over and got you sacked, correct?"

"I quit." Camille squared her shoulders. "And never gave it a second thought. It's not like I used to date him. Unlike some of us." She looked pointedly at Pauley.

"That was ages ago. We were barely out of school."

"There you have it," Keir told Jem with satisfaction. "They're all suspects except for me and Posh. We have no motive. You can eliminate the two of us right now."

Isolde stared at him. Even Trevor, who'd self-consciously swiped at his hair when Keir called him out, looked up in amazement. Camille's ingratiating grin turned mean.

"But you have to know what he was going to do to you, once he got a taste," she said.

Posh looked at the floor, but Keir only looked confused. "What?"

Chuckling, Mrs. Jones elbowed Mrs. Morton, who let out a sudden laugh like the *caw* of a crow.

"He doesn't know," Mrs. Jones said.

"He has no idea," Mrs. Morton said, laughing louder.

"You people are jealous. That's it. Jealous, the lot of you," Keir said.

Rushing to her husband's defense, Posh shrilled, "Your food causes cancer. It causes diabetes and Alzheimer's and arthritis. You might think it tastes better, but the joke's on you. That taste you're addicted to is *poison*."

"Remember, this is about solving a murder," Jem said, trying to dial back the temperature. "If you would all just collect your desserts, we'll—"

"Collect it?" Keir strode to the trolley, snatching up the box marked DARDEN. "Collect this."

Jem got a glimpse of the cake—layers of unfrosted yellow sponge spackled together with gluey muesli—before he heaved it at the wall. It hit with a splat. Clumps of muesli went everywhere. The individual sponge layers landed on the carpet intact. One of them bounced.

"Come along, Portia," Keir sniffed.

Before they were out of earshot, Mrs. Jones asked Mrs. Morton, "What do you reckon it tasted like?"

Mrs. Morton smiled. "Arse."

13

A FRAUD, A WITCH, AND A MISSION OF MERCY

"You expect me to allow poisoned food in my kitchen?" The Bay View's chef de cuisine glared incredulously at Jem, hands on hips. "The culinary staff is already being maligned by idiots who believe in a Mad Poisoner"—she infused the words with a remarkable nasal emphasis—"and now you *want* to give them a reason to be afraid?"

"They're already running scared," Jem said. "Between what happened to Sergeant Hackman and what happened to Lemmy, most of the guests seem to have shifted to a liquid diet. Which they're supplementing with packets of crisps. I really don't think you'll have many takers in the dining room tonight."

"It's true," Gregory told the chef. "When I went out to look at the storm, I passed the gift shop. The pegboard of crisps and energy bars is cleaned out. Even the candy is gone, apart from some wine gums and ring pops."

"Guests of this hotel would rather eat *crisps* than my food?" Aghast, the chef de cuisine glared at the Bake Off contestants who'd filed in behind Jem, each carrying a boxed dessert. "*Non.* Find another place. If you try and store them here, you'll find them left in the rain. Like that song, 'MacArthur Park.'" She let out a ringing *hon-hon-hon*.

"Wow." Pauley, the last of the group, entered the kitchen carrying Clarence's black and gold box. She gazed at the chef for a few seconds, saying nothing. Slowly, she approached the haughty figure in her towering white toque, until they were mere inches apart.

"Hello." Pauley tilted her head to one side. "And your name is...?"

"Rose-Fleur Legrendre. Chef de cuisine." Rose-Fleur lifted her chin. "Graduate of *L'Atelier des Sens, s'il vous plaît*."

"Is that so? Well. I see you've met my friend, Jem Jago. My very best friend. Also, a graduate of St. Mary's School. Go Lionfish. Jem needs you to store this evidence in your freezer. And your answer is...?"

"But of course," Rose-Fleur said almost meekly. "Gregory, assist them. I need a cigarette." Turning on her heel, she entered the scullery. This time, Jem noticed, she didn't open the door just wide enough to slip inside. She banged through carelessly, stalked past the dishwashing apparatus, and burst through the door at the other end.

"What was that?" she muttered to Pauley, who only shook her head.

Storing the evidence only took a few minutes. Gregory found a roll of blank stickers, wrote POISON in black marker on each, and as the entries went into the freezer, he gave each a sticker and tucked them in an out-of-the-way place.

"Will the evidence be safe here?" Pauley asked.

"I think so. I usually leave the freezer unlocked all day, but from now until the police collect these, I'll keep it locked," Gregory said. He seemed far less nervous than he had when Jem first questioned him alongside Sebastian Minting. "Won't be an inconvenience since we can't expect much demand for dinner or breakfast."

"I wouldn't be too sure about that," Pauley said. "Bad enough we're all trapped here without WiFi. Not to mention all the crisps are gone. But never fear, I'll bet your boss and I can dream something up. Where does she go to smoke?"

Gregory looked startled.

"She wouldn't want me to—"

"This is official business," Jem put in, with all the menace an unpaid amateur sleuth could muster. Fortunately, Gregory seemed easily intimidated.

"She's gone to the smoking area. Go through that scullery and out the back door." Gregory pointed. "Walk down the corridor until you reach a fire door with an electronic lockset. The exit code is 111. If she asks, you heard it from someone else. I mean it, or you might have another murder on your hands."

Pauley patted his forearm reassuringly. "Don't worry. She won't be mad. I have some great ideas to get everyone fed, I promise."

Once they'd passed through the scullery and into the long white corridor that was clearly meant for staff only, the rain on the roof sounded much louder. The howling wind could be heard, too, as if only a few inches of brick and drywall separated them from the storm.

"Spill it," Jem told Pauley. "Is the chef a fraud?"

"You caught that, huh?" Pauley grinned.

"I noticed you asked her name, but she didn't ask yours. And her French accent is straight out of *Monty Python*."

"Yeah. It's Abigail Hibbert. From St. Mary's School? She was a year behind us."

Jem tried to remember. They'd walked several yards before a vague impression came to her: a quiet, mousy-haired girl who never took off her headphones. "Are you sure?"

"Of course, I'm sure. She's dyed her hair red and she's wearing green contact lenses, but it's Abbie. Pretty brill of her to reinvent herself as an authentic French chef."

"I'll say."

"I'll bet she has one of the best paying jobs in the islands. And St. Martin's is so insulated, if she stays in char-acter—and in the kitchen—I doubt anyone will recognize her. Which is good, because she'd be out on her *derriere*, full stop, if Fernsby found out his chef de cuisine is a fake."

"You think so?"

"You don't?"

"When Fernsby was hiding behind that column in Reception, he only revealed himself when someone insulted the eggs Benedict," Jem said. "And when I met with him in his office, he mentioned he'd only given a key to the chef. Then he said he trusted her completely." She shook her head. "But none of that matters now. You seem to remember Abbie better than I do. Do you think she might poison someone?"

Pauley looked flummoxed. "After watching those bakers rip each other apart, don't you think we have enough suspects with motive and opportunity?"

"Sure, but a person maintaining a great job under false pretenses rings all kinds of alarms. And if anyone has unusual access and expertise when it comes to food, it's Abbie."

"Rose-Fleur," Pauley corrected. "We have to call her by her new name, so we don't accidentally grass. Listen. I know she's technically being deceptive, but chef de cuisine at a place like this is a big deal. If she's done the job for more than a week and hasn't embarrassed herself, she's competent. And she's a fellow Scillonian who's just trying to get along. We can't throw her under the bus. Not unless she gives us good reason."

They were within sight of the door Gregory described when they heard footsteps pattering behind them—someone coming at a run. Instantly imagining the ragged person in the flapping brown coat, or perhaps the mysterious hoodie-clad doorknob-jiggler, Jem spun around. It was another heart-pounding moment when she wished she had the foresight to go about with a Kevlar vest under her shirt and one of those 140 dB personal alarms. Or perhaps just a sturdy umbrella with a good sharp point.

But it was fortunate she had none of those things, because the person running after them down the hall was Agnetha, the bead-sweeper and check-in clerk. And she already looked scared to death.

"Ms. Jago! Wait. Ms. Jago!"

Agnetha came skidding up, so that Jem and Pauley had to catch and steady her to keep her from tumbling over. Once she'd caught her breath, she asked all in a rush, "Did the Bake Off judge die?"

"Yes," Jem said. Had Fernsby made an announcement? That seemed unlikely. Perhaps the same grapevine that had spread rumors about the Mad Poisoner had also disseminated news of Lemmy's death.

"Is it murder?" Agnetha asked.

"Well, I can't be sure yet, but it seems like it. Why? Do you know something?"

"Yes. I had a dream last night. About a woman dead in a stairwell."

"You said that earlier," Jem said. "Except—not quite that. You said you dreamed about a woman on the floor."

"On the floor of a stairwell," Agnetha said. "On the landing between flights."

"That's creepy," Pauley said. "But what does it have to do with Lemmy's murder?"

"I don't know." Agnetha bit her lip. "I don't go around grassing on people. I live and let live. I'm not a gossiper." She sounded as if she were arguing herself out of some action she'd nearly convinced herself to take.

"Agnetha," Jem said. "Do you think maybe there's a good reason you've been dreaming about death? That maybe you've caught wind of something in your waking life? A person acting suspiciously, or doing something you find untrustworthy?"

The young woman nodded.

"You know, when Hack collapsed, it scared me to death. I ran around looking for the first aid kit. I had to scream at Xavier. That struck me as pretty weird," Jem said.

Agnetha said nothing.

"Was he hiding it? Deliberately making sure that if someone needed help, they couldn't get it?"

The younger woman's discomfort rippled up through her body. Balancing on the sides of her feet, she twisted her fingers together and shook strands of fine brown hair out of her eyes.

"Agnetha?"

"I'm not a gossiper. Or a mind reader," she replied at last.

"After I gave Hack the medicine and he started coming out of it, you dedicated yourself to gathering your beads," Jem continued. "Other people were watching Hack, wondering if he was really okay. You never looked at us.

Even when asked a direct question, you kept your attention on those beads."

"I'm shy," Agnetha whispered.

"Shy? Or guilty?" Jem folded her arms across her chest. "Fernsby told me Xavier probably nicked your beads to teach you a lesson. That's one possibility. The other is, you two have something going on. Teasing, romancing behind the scenes—"

"I would never," Agnetha broke in, eyes wide.

"I'm just looking for a reasonable scenario," Jem said inexorably. Her instincts told her the young woman was involved somehow. The aura of guilt was palpable. "Where were those other poisonings on St. Martin's?" she asked Pauley.

"King Triton's."

"Right. Did you work there, Agnetha? You'd better tell me the truth. I *will* find out."

"No," Agnetha said, finally showing a bit of spirit. "Xavier did, but not me."

"Well, maybe the bad seafood was down to him," Jem said. "Maybe it was deliberate. And maybe when he moved to Bay View and started serving wine, he decided to put something toxic in the lemon water, hide the first aid kit, and watch the fun."

"Maybe to impress you," Pauley suggested.

"He didn't. And I don't know anything about what happened to the policeman. It must have been a freak accident," Agnetha cried.

"But do you know what happened to Lemmy Beagle-hole?" Jem shot back. "You must, or you wouldn't have dashed this way to ask me about it."

"I don't know anything for certain," Agnetha said, fingers twisting again. "I won't accuse anyone without proof. You have to be careful how you treat people, or it rebounds on you, three times as hard."

"Just tell me what you suspect," Jem urged, now truly intrigued. "I'll sniff around and see if the idea holds water."

"I can't. People will say I'm out for revenge. And I'm not," Agnetha said, backing away. "I'm sorry. I see now I shouldn't have bothered you."

"I really think you should just tell me," Jem said again. "I promise I'll be discreet."

"Sorry." Turning, Agnetha launched herself, running headlong back the way she'd come.

"Bet you could catch her," Pauley said as the young woman rounded a corner out of sight.

"Ten years ago, sure. She runs like a gazelle." Jem looked at her friend. "What do you think that was all about?"

Pauley shrugged. "I'd be lying if I didn't say she seems a bit *away with the fairies*."

"Yes, but she is an employee. She must see a lot."

"Sure. But based on everything we've learned so far, I figure Isolde's cake was poisoned by someone with access to her ingredients," Pauley said. "You heard her say she's a professional who doesn't lick the spoon. Someone might have laced her flour with who knows what, and she never realized it. Which is why I always lick the spoon."

"I thought someone probably poisoned the cake while it was left in her unlocked shop," Jem said. "But that seems to go along with the Mad Poisoner theory, which I hate. How can I deduce a person who poisons at random?"

"Maybe Isolde did it herself *but* thought Lemmy would die a few hours after sampling various cakes. Meaning she fingered herself unknowingly," Pauley said.

"Not bad. You could be onto something." Jem sighed.

"But now I can't stop thinking about Agnetha. I should really go after her and try again, shouldn't I?"

"Go," Pauley agreed. "I'll see what Rose-Fleur is willing to tell us out of gratitude for keeping her secret. Then we'll compare notes."

Agnetha really did run like a gazelle, leaving Jem in the dust. She'd probably taken an alternate route back to the hotel proper. The Bay View wasn't huge, but to Jem, every option looked the same: an unmarked white corridor. Retracing her steps seemed easiest, and when she emerged from the scullery back into the kitchen, she found the staff on a break. The half-prepped food was now covered with upside-down bowls and cheesecloths.

"We don't know if we're meant to carry on with the original menu," Gregory said. "Did you find Chef?"

"No, but my friend Pauley's on it," Jem said. "Enjoy your downtime while you can."

From the staging room, she crossed into Ballroom A, which was now deserted apart from two corpses: Lemmy under his tablecloth, and the cake Keir had heaved at the wall.

Maybe we should store Lemmy in the kitchen freezer, too, Jem thought, marveling at herself for not thinking of it sooner. *But not until Pauley and Rose-Fleur get dinner sorted.*

From Ballroom A, she made her way to Decant Resist, which still had a few patrons, all of whom looked half in the bag. At the counter, Xavier was counting his tips. Those crocheted *Star Wars* figures she'd knocked over had been restored to their proper places. She picked one up, studying it as she asked,

"Xavier? Can I talk to you for a minute?"

"On a break," he said, tucking the notes away.

"This won't take long. I wanted to ask you about—"

"On a break," he repeated obstinately, striding past her into the men's lavatory.

Jem followed him—a murder investigation was no time to observe the social niceties—but the lavatory must have been a one-seater, because she heard the loud *click* of a lock. She could still shout questions at him through the door, but was he likely to answer?

I can't see how he had anything to do with Lemmy's death. He was serving drinks in Decant Resist the whole time Mrs. Jones was on the floor. So, if Isolde is innocent, and someone messed about with her cake while she was gone, it physically couldn't have been Xavier, she thought.

The water, though—that's a different story. Fernsby said Xavier lives for his tips, and he'd obviously made a pretty penny so far today. Could he have put something in the water to put a bad taste in peoples' mouths, so they'd come buy from him? That sounds mad. I'm grasping at straws.

In the common area, the glass water decanter had been taken away. It was also deserted, apart from Camille, who was scribbling into a notebook, and Posh, who was flipping through an old issue of *Scillonian*. It was the first time Jem had ever seen her without her husband. If she was aware of Jem, she gave no sign. As for Camille, she glanced up and winked. Jem couldn't help noticing that she was writing with a fancy gel pen—pink, to match her hair.

I've actually spawned an imitator, she thought. But her current gel pen's color was Tremendous Teal, so at least there was that difference.

Reception was dark, bereft of Agnetha or anyone else. Hack had asked that everyone lucky enough to have rooms stay confined in them. It was safer than letting people roam at will, especially if the Mad Poisoner theory was true.

Although curious how Hack was feeling, she couldn't go up to the room yet, because she'd forgotten to ask Pauley which room number.

I can't be the only one who's gotten confused. Maybe something similar happened to the man in the hoodie. Maybe he's not an interloper at all, Jem thought.

Except he ran when the Mintings challenged him, she reminded herself. *And Fernsby noticed a hoodie was missing from his lost-and-found pile. So was the pink hat. Which probably means Brown Coat and Mr. Hoodie both raided the box and are working together in some way.*

Giving up on Xavier, Jem wandered over to Kestrel & Peregrine, the sprawling restaurant that accounted for up to half the ground floor. It was dim and deserted, most of the chairs stacked neatly atop their tables. In one corner sat a baby grand piano. At the rear of the dining room, floor-to-ceiling windows overlooked the sea. Storm Veronica was out there, and she was spectacular. The waves were huge, cresting to terrible heights and then crashing against the rocks. In the distance, black clouds pulsed against the gray, lit from within. The storm's worst fury wasn't upon them yet. When it arrived, it would be electric.

Within sight of the empty maître d's podium was the Bay View's gift shop, which had been plundered to near nonexistence. All the magazines and newspapers were gone, along with most of the paperback novels. A sizable chunk of children's books and soft toys were missing, too, considering that Jem had seen only two kiddies among the guests. As *boulanger* Gregory had said, the pegboard of snacks was completely wiped out. The refrigerated case of bottled water and sodas was empty, too.

A passage at the gift shop's rear lead somewhere else. Curious, Jem entered to discover the Bay View's boutique library. After perusing the hotel website, she'd been excited to see it. But the reality didn't live up to the ad copy.

"Audacious, weren't they? To bill this pile of trash as a library?" Sebastian Minting said by way of greeting. He sat in a club chair with a closed book—*The Organized Mind*, by Daniel J. Levitin—on his lap.

"Dad has opinions," Jace said. He, too, was settled in a club chair, but his choice—a coffee table book about cars of the 1950s—was open to a picture of a 1959 Mini.

"So do I," Jem admitted. "When I heard the Bay View had a library, I didn't expect the Long Room at Trinity College, but I didn't expect a remainders table, either. How are you feeling, Jace?"

The young man smiled. "That obvious, eh?"

"You're still a bit green."

"Witnessing a murder will do that," Minting said, though with less of his old asperity. "I took a peek out the restaurant's window not long ago. There's every reason to hope the storm will break soon."

As an islander, Jem didn't agree. She wouldn't bet on the winds to die down before dawn. But correcting this man's rare moment of optimism seemed unkind.

Jace, suddenly pale, sucked in his breath. His trembling hands jerked, knocking the car book to the floor.

"Son. It's all right. It's all right," Minting said, hurrying to Jace and holding his hands to bolster him against the tremors.

Jem's stomach dropped. This wasn't just serious. This was acute.

"Mr. Minting. What kind of medicine is your son overdue for?"

"His bloody insulin," Minting snapped. "His idiot brother removed Jace's backup case from our luggage. To make room for his Xbox, don't you know? On vacation, we usually bring extra insulin. Thanks to Nigel, we ran out yesterday. I may never forgive him."

"Let it go," Jace whispered, his trembling abating. "I'm responsible for my own meds. This time I didn't check because I got lazy. I assumed if I ran out, I could always dash over to Boots and get a refill."

"Could someone in the hotel have insulin to share?" Jem asked.

"Oh, what a brilliant idea. Thanks for that." Minting glared at her. "It never would have occurred to me to—"

"Dad." Jace's soft voice cut through his father's rant. "Stop shouting. Please."

Minting cleared his throat. Tears of helpless fury stood in his eyes.

"Forgive me, Ms. Jago. Yes, we have asked. There are no other insulin-dependent people here. In case someone was stonewalling, I offered ten thousand pounds on the spot for enough vials to get Jace through. No takers." He wiped his eyes. "If you aren't familiar with diabetic hyperosmolar syndrome, it goes like this. Nausea, seizures, coma, and death."

"Right," Jem murmured. A single possibility came to her, but it was a thin reed at best. "Try and keep your spirits up until I come back. I have one card to play. Cross your fingers that it pays out."

14

OF PIPS AND PITS

Pauley waved away Abbie's—make that Rose-Fleur's—
second offer of a hit off her cigarette. Funny how quickly
you slide back into the attitudes and habits of childhood
when reunited as adults. In Pauley's rebellious, disobeying-
teachers-behind-the-football-pitch phase, she'd occasionally
shared purloined smokes with her schoolmates, including
Rose-Fleur. Now that they were all grown up, that easy inti-
macy had faded, and Rose-Fleur seemed to know no other
way to relate.

They weren't in the Bay View's designated smoking
area; it was located outside. But they were as close as possible, in a glass vestibule not far from the generator room,
overlooking the courtyard. It gave a good view of the storm,
or a daunting one, depending on how you looked at it.

"You guys bunk out there?" Pauley asked, squinting at a
low outbuilding on the courtyard's far side. The courtyard
itself was raised, but the rainwater drained over the side,
swamping the bushes and sending the runoff downhill.

"Yes. As chef de cuisine, I have my own little room.
Everyone else sleeps dormitory-style," Rose-Fleur replied.

"I wish I could get over there for a change of clothes. Sleeping in my whites won't be comfortable."

"Not worth the risk," Pauley said. The courtyard's concrete picnic tables were still in place, but their half-moon benches had been toppled by the wind. The big canvas umbrellas were a total loss; two were turned inside-out, metal ribs snapped, while another had been blown away. Near the dormitory, a tree was down, and the water was rising. When the employees returned to their quarters, they might find them flooded.

"I don't usually smoke on duty," Rose-Fleur said, still employing a soft French accent, perhaps out of habit. "But being recognized came as a shock. I need the nicotine."

"This isn't worth getting your toque and coat all fumey. I didn't follow you here to threaten blackmail," Pauley said. "I just want to pick your brains about Lemmy's murder."

"I thought your friend was the sleuth."

"She is, but we're working together."

Rose-Fleur regarded her silently for a moment, then said, "You might as well know. I think it's quite possible the poisoner works for me."

"What? Who?"

"I don't know who. It only occurred to me just now." The chef took a final deep drag on her cigarette. "I started here about six months ago. I ran out of tuition money before I could finish my culinary training, but I really believed I was ready for prime time, so I made up a new persona and went for it. Talk about a shock.

"Running a kitchen on this level is harder than I ever dreamed. At first, I could barely keep up. But I made it," Rose-Fleur said proudly. "Mr. Fernsby loves my work. Maybe I wasn't a true chef de cuisine when I started, but I am now." She stubbed out her cigarette to drive the point home.

"The first time I noticed something strange going on was in October. There was a casual restaurant that used to operate on St. Martin's, not far from the Bay View—"

"King Triton's," Pauley broke in. "Jem and I were just talking about it. I for one was sorry to see it go."

"Well, it was nothing special, but it was good plain food. Everyone at the Bay View ate there from time to time, just to get off the premises for an hour. But one day in October, half the people who ate lunch at King Triton's took sick. Nothing terrible, just indigestion. The next day, the same thing happened, only worse. Three people went to hospital and one had to have their stomach pumped. That was Agnetha, our check-in clerk."

"I've talked to her briefly," Pauley said cautiously. "You heard this directly from her?"

Rose-Fleur nodded. "I've taken her under my wing. I mean, as much as I can, given that she's in Hospitality and I rarely leave the kitchen. She's been bullied from the moment she turned up. She's shy, and unusual. Plus, there was the smudging incident..."

"Smudging?" Pauley frowned. "You mean, like, with burning sage?"

"Exactly. On her first day, five minutes after she clocked in, Agnetha smudged the bottom floor of the hotel with a bowl of burning sage. *Everything* stank. The smell lingered for hours, and the guests were furious. I came out of my kitchen ready to throw a fit that would make Gordon Ramsay blush. But when I saw poor little Agnetha in her secondhand suit, I couldn't do it. I ended up convincing Mr. Fernsby to give her another chance."

"Why on earth would she do something like that?" Pauley asked.

"Because she's New Age-y and she believes in all that crystal/dreamcatcher stuff. Also, she didn't want to get her stomach pumped again. Because after King Triton's closed, the bartender got a job here, in Food Service."

"Xavier," Pauley said. So at least that much from Agnetha had been accurate.

"Exactly, Xavier. Agnetha confided something in me. She's convinced he was behind the whole thing at King Triton's. They were together at St. Mary's School, and he made her life hell. She thinks he not only poisoned the food but gave her an extra dose. After all," Rose-Fleur said, "of all the casualties, her case was the worst."

Pauley considered this. She didn't have to ask why Agnetha, having years of unhappy school memories associated with Xavier, would take a job at the Bay View knowing he was there. As Jem and any Scillonian jobseeker could tell you, good positions in the islands were rare. And so, despite the suspicions Agnetha had confided to Rose-Fleur, she'd been willing to work alongside her tormenter.

"That's interesting. But did Agnetha have any proof that Xavier did it? I'm thinking she couldn't have, or she would have gone to the police."

"No proof. Just a hunch based on his character. And the fact that his favorite bar clients didn't get ill. Xavier lives for his tips. He'd never jeopardize them."

"When you said the poisoner worked for you, did you mean Xavier? Based on Agnetha's suspicions?"

Rose-Fleur shook her head. "I think the poisoner works for me because of things I witnessed. Last month, while doing a kitchen spot check, I discovered a handful of apple pips boiling in a soup pot. Everyone swore they knew nothing about it.

"Last week, I accidentally binned a spatula. It was a good one I couldn't spare, so I stormed out to the dumpster to get it back. While I was rooting around in there, I found the meat of twenty peaches tossed in. No pits. Just the edible parts."

"That's weird. Why would someone want the pits?"

"Because they're poisonous." Rose-Fleur seemed amazed that Pauley didn't know that. "For centuries, people were afraid of peaches. The ancient Romans used to execute prisoners with a decoction of peach pits."

"Pauls! There you are." Jem came skidding around a corner into the vestibule. She was panting and in full Scilly Sleuth mode, as Pauley called it. Which meant she looked slightly mad.

"Perfect timing. Riddle me this: what does apple pips, King Triton's and peach pits have—"

"Forget all that. Who on St. Martin's takes insulin?"

Pauley blinked. "No one. I mean, Emily Church used to, but she changed to an insulin pump."

Jem groaned. "There's no one else on the island? You're absolutely sure?"

"Well, in Hugh Town there's—"

"We can't get to Hugh Town," Jem cut across her, looking madder still. "Jace Minting desperately needs injectable insulin. He could lapse into a coma at any minute. He might even die. Is there anyone on St. Martin's who could treat him? A retired doctor or a nurse?"

"How do you expect her to know that?" Rose-Fleur asked. "I've been here six months and I don't know."

"Yes, well, I'm a Gwyn," Pauley said, thinking fast. "I remember now—Emily's pump procedure was postponed.

The rescheduled date might not have come round yet. She could still be injecting insulin daily."

Jem grabbed her by the shoulders and gave her a joyous little shake. "I knew it! If anyone had the answer, it would be you. Now. How far away does Emily live?"

"In Middle Town. This is Low Town. So maybe a mile away."

"More like half a mile," Rose-Fleur said. "An easy walk if not for..." She tailed off, gesturing toward the windows. Outside on the flooded lawn, the missing umbrella canvas chose that moment to reappear, cartwheeling past the glass to prove Storm Veronica's fury. Reading Jem's face, she added, "You can't go out there. You'll be struck by lightning or blown off your feet."

"I'll chance it," Jem said.

"And you won't be alone. I might get struck by lightning," Pauley admitted, "but no wind has knocked me down yet."

After a hurried conversation, Pauley and Jem decided the best way forward was just to do it. If they stopped to inform Hack, Micki, or anyone else, time would be wasted as the storm intensified. As for telling the Minting family, they decided not to. Suppose Emily wasn't at home, or had already received her pump? It would be doubly cruel to raise Jace's hopes, only to come back and yank the rug out.

Since neither Pauley nor Jem had been wise enough to bring their heaviest macs, Rose-Fleur agreed to let them into the employees' cloakroom.

"Just let me take a peek first. Someone might be inside, expecting privacy."

That made no sense to Pauley, but rather than waste time objecting, she stepped back, allowing Rose-Fleur to crack open the door and slip inside. After half a minute, the chef opened the door wide.

"All clear! Come pick a coat. Sorry, but there doesn't seem to be any boots or brollys. No hats, either."

"This one has a hood." Jem pulled out a man's red and green plaid raincoat. "Ugly, isn't it? Smells of dog, too."

Pauley stared at the coat. She recognized it. Not just the pattern but it specifically. Impossible that such a hideous item had a twin anywhere in the world, much less the Isles of Scilly.

"What? You look like you've seen a ghost," Jem said. Rose-Fleur was watching her, too.

"No. Only, there are more people with bad taste in the islands that I ever realized." She slipped into a yellow slicker as Jem tried on the plaid raincoat. "Tell me the plan again?"

Jem grinned. "Run like hell."

15

INTO THE STORM

Jem's choice of the dog-scented coat proved good protection. If only she had a waterproof balaclava to shield her face from the rain, which pounded down from all directions—east, north, west, and outer space. The drops were big, forceful, and cold as ice. As she and Pauley exited the Bay View Hotel, the wind came howling up from the quay, smelling and tasting of salt water. As for running like hell, it was easier said than done. Even walking like heck was difficult.

"Oh!" Stumbling, Pauley laughed as a gust blew up her skirt. "This is going to change my attitude toward trousers." Sliding on the muddy lawn, she narrowly righted herself before falling. "And granny boots."

"Take my hand," Jem said.

With fingers interlaced and heads together, they pressed on, a solid front against Storm Veronica's onslaught.

"What's the story with the chef?"

"The what?"

"The chef," Jem bellowed. Pauley grinned at her, and she understood. For hours they'd been conferring in mutters, trapped in the suspect-filled fishbowl that was the Bay View. Now, out in the storm, there was no longer any reason to keep their voices down.

"Rose-Fleur's on the level," Pauley said. "What she told me made me suspect Xavier."

Jem listened to the story of Agnetha and Xavier's lingering animosity, the smudging debacle, the King Triton poisonings, and Rose-Fleur's discovery of the pips and pits. Various threads were coming together, if not without gaps. When Agnetha stopped Jem and nearly unloaded her suspicions, she was almost surely about to accuse Xavier. As for Decant Resist's first-aid-kit-hiding ginger, his behavior made sense if he had a penchant for poisoning.

"That's interesting, but it doesn't tie into what happened to Lemmy. Wasn't Xavier on shift while Isolde was away from her bakery? How could he—"

Jem broke off as her foot slipped on mud as slick as ice. Anyone else would have been dragged down with her, but Pauley held firm, refusing to budge, and saving Jem from a mud bath.

"Upsy-daisy. Remember what I said about someone poisoning Isolde's pantry? Maybe Xavier has a taste for mayhem now, and he's sprinkling it wherever he can to cause chaos. Which would make Lemmy collateral damage. Just another victim of the Mad Poisoner."

"It's possible. But I don't believe it," Jem said. "Everyone despised Lemmy. Even you and Micki would be prime suspects if I didn't know for sure you're not murderers. I refuse to believe he died just because he was unlucky."

"There's our path ahead." Pauley tightened her grip on Jem's hand. "We can try it, but it's flooding. And I don't like how fast the water's moving. Let's go up this hill instead."

"Too steep," Jem said.

"We can make it. It's a shortcut."

"I don't know..." Jem began, but Pauley was already yanking her hand, dragging her forward.

"What happened to the crazy Jemmie I grew up with?"

"She's afraid of breaking a hip."

Bent against the wind, Jem and Pauley picked their way up the sharp ascent. Halfway to the top, one of Pauley's granny boots shot out from under her. Her echoing shriek sounded like a banshee.

"Pauls? Are you okay? *Pauls?*"

Her friend was on her back, skirt up and black lace tights taking in water. Gritting her teeth, Jem tried to haul her upright. For a moment, they seemed on the verge of victory. Then Jem's muddy trainers slipped out from under her. Down the hill they went in a rolling tangle of limbs, shrieking all the way.

Back where we started, Jem thought, face down in the muddy grass. Above her, the heavens continued their cosmic beatdown, most of it missing Jem. She was shielded by Pauley, who'd landed on top of her.

"Get—off—" Jem gasped.

"Stupid bloody boots!"

The crushing weight on top of Jem shifted. Raising her face, she saw a black projectile arc through the air. Turning her face up so the rain could wash it clean, she watched Pauley's other granny boot fly past.

"Are you hurt?" Jem gasped.

"Only my pride." Feet clad only in wet tights, Pauley arose shakily like some kind of allegory—womankind's triumph over the forces of darkness, perhaps. "Power of yoga. I can take a fall."

"Maybe, but you can't go on shoeless," Jem shouted over

the wind. "Point me to Emily's cottage and I'll find it myself."

"I'd never leave you to go alone. I've seen you trip over the pattern in a rug," Pauley retorted. "Now that I'm barefoot, I'll be fine. But the minute we get back, I'm taking a hot bubble bath."

"Me, too. I'm freezing."

Locking hands, they attempted the hill again. This time they succeeded. At the top, they saw lashing trees, downed limbs, and a spreading water meadow. In the distance was a small shop with a cottage next door.

"Is that Cake Me Proud?"

"Yeah. Let's head for the porch. Take a breather from the storm."

As Pauley launched herself into the wind, Jem was pulled along with her. Over the sea, lightning flashed and thunder boomed, but somehow they kept their feet, soon finding themselves under the partial shelter of Cake Me Proud's shingled porch.

"Isolde left the lights on," Pauley said. "How can she still have power?"

Jem peered through the shop door's window. "It's a torch. No, a battery lantern. Sitting on top of the—*oh*." She ducked out of sight. "Somebody's inside."

"Did you get a look?"

"It was someone small. Maybe a child."

"I hope a kid wasn't caught out alone in the storm. Let's check on them," Pauley said, trying the handle. It opened, revealing a showroom that offered baking equipment, prepackaged goodies, coffee, tea, and Keir Darden, all five feet of him, standing behind the empty pastry case with a lantern in his hand.

"What are you doing here?" he demanded. Like them, he had wet hair, wet skin, and a dripping wet mac.

"We might ask you the same question. Looking for something, Keir?" Jem asked.

"Investigating the scene of the crime. Hackman's in no shape to do it, and I refuse to let the killer get away scot-free."

"Investigating? You have to know you can't be in here. The police will want to go through this place with a fine-tooth comb. Your fingerprints and DNA will only muddle things." Jem issued the speech with authority; she'd been on the receiving end of it often enough.

"You're just afraid of being shut out," Keir said. "I get it. But I only want justice served. Come around the counter into the kitchen and see what I found."

Isolde's bakery kitchen was white and probably spotless, though Jem could only focus on it piecemeal, in lantern-illuminated bites. The stainless-steel worktables were mostly bare, no pans or tools out of place, except for a pair of plastic tongs. Keir led Jem and Pauley to an uncovered bin by the rear door, aiming his lantern so they could see inside.

Only one thing was inside. A mailing envelope, standard size and dusty mauve in color, decorated by golden curlicues and cabbage roses.

"I used those tongs to examine it. Give it a sniff," Keir said.

Jem dug in her trouser pocket, located Minting's handkerchief—miraculously still dry—and used it to pick up the tongs. She didn't have to put the unmarked, unsealed envelope close to her face to register the scent.

"Almonds."

"Right. And you know what smells of almonds?" Keir said. "Cyanide."

"True." Jem looked down at the little man, regarding him curiously. "Weren't you the one accusing other people of knowing too much about poisons?"

He waved that away. "Everyone knows about cyanide. What matters is this. Isolde put cyanide in her cake. She just forgot to conceal the envelope that contained the powder."

"Right. And she cleaned up her kitchen but left the smoking gun in the bin for all to see."

Keir shrugged. "Criminals make mistakes. That's how they're caught."

"You don't know it's Isolde's envelope. It's quite old-fashioned," Jem said. "Maybe it belongs to Mrs. Jones or Mrs. Morton."

"No, it's hers." Grinning, Keir pointed at the door. "That leads into the house. I took a quick peek in Isolde's bedroom. Fan of steamy reads, that one. And on her desk is her stationery set. Cabbage roses and all."

"You went in her bedroom?" Pauley said, appalled.

"I investigated," Keir retorted. "I don't believe for a minute that you two haven't done the same."

Jem and Pauley, swapping glances, decided to let that pass.

Keir said, "If you don't believe me, look at this." Pulling his mobile from his coat's inner pocket, he showed them the latest picture on his photo roll: Isolde's roll-top desk, with a Victorian-style blotter, quill pen, and that distinctive, dusty mauve stationery.

"Fine." Removing her own mobile, Jem took a shot of the envelope. "I'll ask her about it when I'm ready. Please don't give her a heads-up. I want to see if she's surprised."

"I won't," Keir said, looking more than a little shifty, "as long as you promise to lean on her hard. At first, I thought it might be Trevor, but now I'm sure it's Isolde. I'd hate to watch a poisoner serving treats to people, day in and day out, always waiting for the other shoe to drop."

"Isn't that how you feel about Isolde's kind of baking, anyway? Cyanide or no?" Pauley asked.

"You might be a little nicer, Pauley. I'm the one with the lantern to lead us back," Keir said.

"We're going the other way," Jem said. "Go on without us. We'll be back as soon as possible."

"The other way? Why?"

"Investigating," Jem lied, enjoying that last look of mystification he threw over his shoulder before leaving. So, he fancied himself a detective, did he? Let him try to work out what the Scilly Sleuth was seeking in Middle Town in the middle of a deluge.

Exiting Cake Me Proud, they pushed on along the path. After a brief respite, the rain felt colder than ever. While they were inside, the sun had set, settling a profound darkness over St. Martin's. Although the Isles of Scilly were famously free of major light pollution, the islands were populated, and handheld torches were frequently glimpsed. On ordinary nights, the effect was magical, like the will-o'-the-wisps of legend. But tonight, there was nothing ahead of them but shivering darkness and the whistling wind.

Their mobile torches helped illuminate the path, but it was still hard going. Jem slipped twice, and Pauley swore loudly after tripping on storm debris. Something squat and gray was ahead of them. As they drew closer, it resolved first into large rectangle, then into a stone cottage with a red door.

Jem rapped it with her knuckles hard enough to wake the dead.

"Who's that?" came an uncertain voice.

"Emily, it's Pauley Gwyn. I need help. Please!"

The red door was replaced by a young woman in pajamas and a chenille robe, holding a thick white candle in her hand. Shielding its flame against the wind, she said, "In you get, you dozy donkeys." As they hurried inside, she added, "What are you thinking, roaming about in this weather?"

"We've come from Bay View. There's a trapped guest in trouble," Pauley began.

"Insulin," Jem cut in. "Please tell me you still inject it."

"Oh. No. Finally got my pump." Emily touched her hip. "No more shots for me. I've passed the trial period, which means St. Mary's Hospital will take back my old injectable supplies. Lucky for you," she continued with a grin, "I haven't returned them yet. Would you like regular, fast-acting, or both?"

16

PERSONS OF INTEREST

Perhaps the most luxurious feature of Pauley's gratis suite was the bathroom. A white-on-white porcelain dream, it featured a large bulb-lit mirror, a clamshell sink, clawfoot tub, and glass shower stall. While Pauley soaked in the tub, mountains of bubbles surrounding her like fluffy clouds around a cherub, Jem consigned her cold, wet, mud-splattered self into a steaming hot shower.

The bathroom's amenities included not only bubble bath, botanical shampoo, and a lavender lotion formulated "by royal appointment," but something Jem had never tried: a shower bomb. The instant hot water hit the aromatic purple tablet, a mix of eucalyptus and spearmint scent arose, tickling Jem's nose and enlivening her. After rinsing the rain out of her hair and scrubbing herself all over, Jem adjusted the shower head to its most powerful setting, closed her eyes, stood beneath it, savoring her and Pauley's triumph.

Returning to the hotel had been easier going, not because Storm Veronica had abated, but because they were overjoyed. Emily had given them loads of leftover diabetic supplies, including glass ampules of insulin, disposable syringes, and superfine needles. The wind was just as fierce and the ground was just as muddy, but somehow they made it back without damaging a single ampule. Probably because Jace needed them to.

When they entered the courtyard, one of the Bay View's side doors opened and Rose-Fleur stuck her head out.

"*La vache!* I'd thought you'd been struck by lightning."

As if on cue, a jagged white line split the sky above them, lighting up the courtyard. The flooded zone around the dormitory had doubled.

"Were you waiting for us?" Pauley asked, ducking inside.

"What else do I have to do?" Rose-Fleur closed the door once Jem, too, was out of the rain. "Pauley, where are your shoes? Your baby toe is bleeding."

It was true. Every step Pauley took on the white-tiled floor left behind a muddy, bloody print.

"No worries, I'm off for my bubble bath. Jem, you do the honors with Jace. Rose-Fleur can walk me upstairs in case I slip in my own blood. And," Pauley said, grinning at the chef, "we can talk about tonight's menu. I realize everyone's spooked, but I think there's a way to keep everyone safely fed."

"Which room?" Jem had shouted at their backs.

"Sorry! 204!"

That question finally answered, Jem headed off in search of Jace. She found the Mintings not where she'd left them, in the so-called library, but in their own suite. The big reveal happened so fast, she now recalled it only as a collage of rapid-fire images. Mrs. Minting opening the door; her husband pacing; Nigel sitting disconsolately on the sofa, still in disgrace. Through a bedroom's open door, Jem spied Jace sitting up in bed, surrounded by pillows. She'd lifted the bag of insulin ampules like a trophy. His answering smile made her heart turn over.

She stayed only long enough to be assured that Emily's supplies met the moment. Apparently, the brands were different, but the formulation was similar enough to be safe and effective. Mrs. Minting tried to thank her, and Nigel did, too, but their naked gratitude was hard to bear. As for the family's intimidating patriarch, he excused himself into another room, from which soon drifted the sound of weeping. Jem wished everyone well and got away fast.

"I can smell eucalyptus," Pauley called from the tub.

Jem, eyes closed, water pounding deliciously over her shoulders and back, moaned in acknowledgement. She didn't want to talk yet, or engage her higher faculties. She wanted five more minutes of perfect luxury.

When she finally emerged from the shower stall, Pauley was still underwater. The cascades of bubbles had melted, and the water was surely lukewarm, but Pauley's smile was pure bliss.

"Tell me again how happy they were."

"Delirious. Over the moon. Especially Mrs. Minting. How's your feet?"

"Only mildly terrible." Pauley lifted one from the water, wiggling her toes. "If we're heroes, and it sounds like we are, it's worth a few cuts and bruises to save Jace from a coma. Besides, I have a bigger problem than sore feet."

"What's that?" Jem began rubbing herself down with a fluffy Egyptian cotton towel.

"I'm hungry. Seriously hungry."

"Me, too." As if to prove her point, Jem's stomach growled in sympathy. "Just not enough to risk eternal rest, and I suspect most people here feel the same way. What idea for dinner did you float to Rose-Fleur?"

"A communal thing. I figured the hotel would have teppanyaki grills for summer," Pauley said. "Turns out it does, and they're indoor-outdoor, so they can be operated in the dining room without dangerous fumes. I told Rose-Fleur that we should have a grill party. Everyone gathers around and watches her cook simple dishes from scratch. Steak fajitas, scrambled eggs, fried rice, and so on. There's nothing to fear if you see everything made out in the open."

"Pauls, that's brilliant." Now wrapped in a bath sheet, Jem used a separate towel to begin the arduous process of drying her hair. Her cardinal rule for long hair was set in stone: never blow dry, always gently towel dry. "What will people drink? The gift shop cooler is empty."

"Well, there's wine, obviously. But Rose-Fleur suggested the self-juicing machines they put out with the morning buffet. Guests can split their own oranges, crush them, and drink pure, fresh juice."

"You're a genius. Seriously."

"Well, we need to get Fernsby on board, obviously. I was a bit worried about asking him, but Rose-Fleur was sure he'd play along. She says he's a good egg." Pauley sat up in the bath. "He's not one of your suspects, is he?"

"No."

"Who is?"

Jem flipped her hair and began drying it upside down. "I need to sit down with a fresh notebook and a gel pen and work that out."

∾

Exiting the bathroom in her Bay View branded terry robe, she found Hack in bed, sitting up. He was on top of the duvet, not tucked in, and still in his uniform, apart from his duty belt, reflective yellow jacket, and shoes. To her relief, the long rest had done him good, and he looked almost normal. His healthy color had returned, though a trace of raised welts were still visible on his cheeks. There was no wheezing to be heard, thank goodness. Someone had supplied him with three bottles of Perrier to keep him hydrated. He was drinking one when she came out.

"A gift from Fernsby." Hack lifted it as if toasting her. "Turned up unasked with water and snacks, asking how I was doing. I guess he thought he might need a friend on the force once the investigation starts."

As he spoke, his eyes skipped over her, touching lightly on her bare legs and shoulders. Though she'd never been less dolled up or pulled together, she suddenly felt special. Desirable.

"That must have been quite the shower," Micki said, sounding as if she'd deliberately stepped on the moment. She was sitting in the corner with a book on her lap, which Jem should have noticed, but didn't.

"Oh. Hiya." Jem forced a smile, realizing that Micki was probably being protective of Rhys, whom she'd come to like very much.

I need to tell her we called it quits, she thought. The prospect felt like a lead weight in her gut. She felt almost lucky to have a murder to focus on. It was far more comfortable.

"What are you reading on your phone?" Jem asked Hack. "Don't tell me the WiFi's back."

"No. I've been rereading my police manuals. They're downloaded on my phone for quick access. Anyway, says here," he consulted his mobile, "that in some cases of latex allergy, certain plants may trigger cross-reactions. These include mulberry, rubber trees, oleander, and hemp."

"What kind of loon would put any of those in lemon water?" Micki asked.

"I don't know. But I know what I need," Jem said, heading for her luggage. "Some dry clothes, a fresh note-book, and a gel pen."

After a ducking into the bathroom to change, Jem sat down at the desk with both implements in front of her.

"Right. Let's see. Suspect number one, by popular demand. The Mad Poisoner." Under that she wrote:

Tall person in brown coat and pink sun hat. Shorter person trying doorknobs in a hoodie. If they both raided the lost-and-found box, they are probably working together in some sense. And how did they gain access to Fernsby's office? Either he forgot to lock up, or Rose-Fleur let them in.

"What about Rose-Fleur as the killer?" Jem asked her friends.

"Is that the chef?" Micki asked.

"Haven't met her," Hack reminded Jem. "Why? What has she said or done to spark your suspicion?"

"Well, when Mr. Minting and I first turned up, she was completely obstructive. If Pauls hadn't come in, I doubt she would have answered a single question. And as it happens, she's not exactly who she says she—"

"Jem!" Pauley barreled out of the bathroom wrapped in a towel, holding it together at the crucial spot with an iron grip. "We promised to be discreet."

"A man is dead," Hack said severely. "If someone's lying about their identity, I need to know."

"Spill, spill," Micki chanted.

"She inflated her credentials," Jem said, giving Pauley an apologetic glance. "And she says she's French, but she's actually from the islands. Pauls and I were at school with her. She used to be Abigail Hibbert, but now she lives under an alias."

"And if Fernsby finds out, she's done for. *In this economy.*" Pauley drew a finger across her throat. "If you don't want that on your conscience, keep schtum about it. Besides, she didn't kill anyone."

"I think she's connected to the interlopers, though," Jem said. "She acted really suspicious about the scullery and the cloakroom. Like she had reason to believe someone was in there."

"Maybe she's soft-hearted," Micki said. "I'd let anyone but Jack the Ripper in from this storm."

"Yes, and you'd say so, wouldn't you?" Hack asked. "Rather than provide them with disguises and let them move around at will?"

"This interloper stuff is a red herring," Pauley announced with surprising certainty. "If we think Lemmy's murderer is at large in the hotel, we're mental to waste time on a couple of randos."

"Wow." Micki blinked at Pauley.

"What do you know?" Jem's radar pinged as she stared at her friend.

"I know she gave me the backstory about what happened at King Triton's," Pauley said stoutly, not giving an inch. "I know she said that last month, someone was making a decoction from apple pips, which is a way to brew poison, in her kitchen. And last week, she found a lot of peaches binned for no reason, with only the pits removed. Why would she implicate someone she supervises, which might rebound on her, when she could have shrugged and kept mum?"

"Fair enough. For the moment," Jem said. "What about her assistant, Gregory? He belongs on the suspect list. He could have passed through the staging area and tampered with the cake."

"But this is ridiculous," Pauley groaned. "No offense, Jem, but think about it. Did any of you really *look* at Isolde's cake before Lemmy cut into it?"

"I did," Micki said. "It looked perfect. Flawless, really."

"Exactly. The appearance of the dessert is forty percent of the judging," Pauley said. "Putting aside all the questions of timing, for someone to tamper with a cake after it got on the trolley—well, I just don't see how it wouldn't be noticed. And Lemmy was behind the curtain with the desserts, most, if not all the time."

"Then I'm with Camille. He poisoned himself," Micki said.

"If there's any man who loved himself too much to do himself harm, it was Lemmy," Pauley said.

"I understand what you're saying about the cake looking untouched, but I've heard of some pretty extreme methods of poison delivery," Hack said. "Usually, it's spy vs. spy stuff, but it happens. Like injecting food via hypodermic needle so the adulteration leaves no visible trace."

"Who goes about with hypodermics at hand?" Micki asked.

"Insulin-dependent diabetics," Jem and Pauley said in unison.

Everyone was silent for a moment.

"You don't think...?" Micki began tentatively.

"No," Jem said firmly. "Pauls, explain your theory about Isolde's pantry."

As Pauley went over the tainted flour/never licks the spoon idea, Jem wrote in her notebook,

> *Isolde Jones's cake was the murder weapon. For that reason, she's the most obvious suspect. But she's also the most counterintuitive because she has so much to lose. King Triton's already closed after bouts of food poisoning. Even a hint of shenanigans would put Cake Me Proud out of business.*

After she read it aloud, Hack said, "In my professional opinion, Isolde's shock and horror was authentic. She seemed genuinely gutted. It's quite likely she's the patsy. Either because her cake was the most opportune to use as a vehicle, or because someone wanted to ruin her."

"I had the same impression," Jem admitted. "But here's a new wrinkle. Keir Darden."

In her notebook, she wrote,

> *Keir and his wife, Posh, were almost certainly due for harsh public words from Lemmy. Posh hasn't behaved in a suspicious manner, per se. (Besides, if she had the brass to kill anyone, she would have done in her hubby long ago.) Keir refused to store his cake in the walk-in freezer. He was the first to start slinging accusations, and he went out in the storm to snoop around Cake Me Proud. He claims to have discovered an envelope belonging to Isolde that contained cyanide.*

After she read that aloud, explaining the specifics of the

distinctive stationery and the almond smell, Micki said, "Stitch up. Has to be. It's too perfect."

"I'm inclined to agree," Hack said. "He risked his life to go to her place and root around in her bedroom to discover this perfectly incriminating evidence? It beggars belief."

"My sentiment exactly. Now, I need to get dressed," Pauley said, retreating to the bathroom. Over her shoulder, she added, "Isolde isn't my favorite person. But this much I know for sure. She's not mocha-vellian. She would never straight up murder a man and then rely on her mad persuasion skills to make us all look elsewhere. And she's a good baker, which means she would never poison her own cake. That goes against the grain."

"I'm sorry, love," Micki called. "What was that fancy word you used?"

"Mocha-vellian. Means sneaky. A schemer."

"I think it means sweet like choccie," Jem said. "But also bracing, like coffee."

Pauley stuck her head out of the bathroom, her damp magenta hair standing up like a steampunk crown. "What are you lot on about? I said Isolde's not mocha... mocky... Oh, hell. What's the word?"

"Matcha-vellian?" Hack asked innocently.

"Each and every one of you knows what I mean." Pauley slammed the bathroom door.

"Fine. I just added the words, 'not Machiavellian.' So much for Isolde. What about her ex-husband, Trevor?" Under his name, Jem wrote,

Trevor, unlike Isolde, is the most intuitive killer. He lost his business thanks to Lemmy, which sent him on a downward spiral, causing him to lose his marriage, too.

"He's the one who stands out to me, if I'm being honest," Hack said. "But then again, I never trust a grown man who won't look me in the eye. Do we have any evidence?"

"None that I've seen yet. Except perhaps opportunity," Jem said. "Isolde told us the door between her home and her bakery is never locked. Mrs. Jones and Mrs. Morton have been best friends for ages. Trev and Isolde have known each other for most of their lives. Even though Isolde claims no one was around when she baked and decorated her entry, I wouldn't be surprised if she forgot or deliberately left out those three. After all, she must trust them completely. Which gives him an in."

"He strikes me as socially challenged," Micki said. "And carrying a torch for his ex. I can't imagine why he'd set up a woman he's probably still in love with."

"Noted. Now for the other contestants." Jem tapped her pen against the desktop. "Right. There's Mrs. Jones."

"Overbearing. Entitled. Got me stranded on this island," Hack said.

"But she didn't enter a dessert," Micki objected.

"I still think she should be a suspect," Hack said.

"There's also Mrs. Morton."

"I saw her reading an Agatha Christie," Pauley called from inside the bathroom. "She's got murder on her mind."

"Fair point," Jem said. "So, that leaves only one baker—"

"Two," Pauley yelled from the bathroom.

"Two," Micki said, incensed. "Camille and me. Don't tell me you forgot me?"

Jem rolled her eyes. "Fine. Micki Latham, a very serious and not at all tongue-in-cheek suspect." Under that she wrote,

The Mickster. Shady AF.

"And last comes Camille Carlisle," Pauley said, emerging from the bathroom in a black A-line dress. "Don't forget to put down that she used to work for *All Things Penzance*. And when Lemmy came onboard, she was sacked. At his request, so the story goes."

"Right. Camille Carlisle. Fancies herself as a bit of a detective." Under that, she wrote,

> *Has lived in the Scillies a relatively short amount of time. May have a motive, like so many people who despised Lemmy, but opportunity is unclear.*

She looked up from her journal. "You know what we've completely failed to address?" She pointed her Tremendous Teal pen at Hack. "What happened to him."

"Sometimes weird things just happen," Hack said fatalistically. "There *is* such a thing as coincidence."

"Maybe. But we're missing something," Jem said, reading over her notes with dissatisfaction. "Maybe it's right under our noses."

"I have the cure. Food," Pauley declared. "I'm off to get the preparations started. When it's time to come downstairs, I'll ring the room phone to let you know. Oh, and Micki? People will need some entertainment. Everyone's wrung out. There's a baby grand piano in the dining room. If I can find someone who plays, you'll do the singing, won't you?"

"You've got to be kidding."

"I'm not. Your greatest critic is dead. Your audience literally can't leave the building. This is your moment." With that, Pauley swept out of the room, leaving Jem and Hack swapping glances, and Micki open-mouthed.

17

TEPPANYAKI

The turnout for Grill Night was one hundred percent. Kestrel & Peregrine's dining room was so full, Jem found herself scanning the tables, expecting to find Hoodie and Brown Coat tucking in along with the rest. Fernsby had allowed his staff to join in, with the exception of the kitchen crew, who had eaten first, during set-up. Xavier and Agnetha shared a table, and were seated beside one another, Jem noted. That didn't seem to square with the backstory Rose-Fleur had given pre-insulin escapade, but Jem had enough experience with schoolyard frenemies to know such roles were fluid. Maybe there was an attraction there, after all.

As she watched, Xavier leaned close to Agnetha, murmuring something for her ears only. The young woman flushed, but whether her reaction indicated pleasure or irritation, Jem didn't know.

After everyone's finished supper, I'll corner Agnetha and try to make her talk, she resolved. *I want to hear the story of King Triton's from her own lips.*

In the center of the dining room, Rose-Fleur stood over

the teppanyaki grill. In a fresh toque and spotless white coat, she charmed the guests as she played grill master, serving mostly steak, eggs, and rice to order. If anyone had serious qualms about ingesting food after Lemmy's demise, the sizzles, pops, and heavenly smells soon won them over.

Joining the queue, Jem watched Isolde and Trevor, who stood side by side, watching Rose-Fleur create heart-shaped rice. Meanwhile, Mrs. Jones was already at the dessert station, where Gregory was popping frozen crème brûlées into his microwave, then caramelizing the tops of the heated ones with his blowtorch.

Mrs. Morton, apparently having finished eating, sat reading her Agatha Christie near the wine station, which Fernsby was working himself. For once, he looked calm and almost at ease. Between pouring glasses of red and white, he watched Rose-Fleur's grill tricks. When she bounced an egg from spatula to spatula, finally sending it to land with a plop into her coat pocket, he applauded.

"Jem," said a weak voice. "Save me."

"Never mind all that," Pauley said, frogmarching Micki past the queue. Pauley wore what she'd intended for tomorrow's outfit—a black polka-dot dress in which the dots were actually tiny skulls—but Micki looked like pure glamor in a black floor-length gown. Had she borrowed it from one of the thwarted travelers? Judging by the way she minced along in pumps Jem didn't recognize, she'd definitely borrowed the shoes, and they were too small. Still, with her storm-frizzed hair tamed by a French braid —Pauley's handiwork—Micki turned heads, and then some.

"Hello, everyone," Pauley said, pausing beside the baby grand piano and smiling around the room. "Thank you so much for coming. All credit to our lovely Mr. Fernsby, who made this Grill Night possible, and the incredible chef de cuisine, Rose-Fleur Legendre."

This prompted genuine applause from everyone, not just Fernsby. Rose-Fleur took a bow.

Micki, momentarily unguarded, began edging away. Catching her hand, Pauley brought her back to the stool and microphone stand that was clearly intended for a vocalist.

"Now, as you see, I've lined up some wonderful entertainment for your digestive pleasure. The only essential I haven't been able to beg, borrow, or steal was a piano player. So, if you're the musical type, now's your time to shine. Micki prefers folk music, but she can sing most anything, if you ask me."

The guests and staff were smiling, ready to be entertained, but no one volunteered to play. Pauley, scanning faces, pointed to Xavier, who was once again whispering to Agnetha.

"Are you a musician? Don't be shy."

"Me? Never." He laughed.

"What about you, love?" she asked Agnetha.

"I could never. Sorry," Agnetha said. Seemingly embarrassed by the attention, she pushed back from the table and exited the dining room.

"Wow, I never meant to cause a mass exodus. Come on, folks. There has to be someone who—"

"Ni-gel. Ni-gel," chanted Jace Minting, who was eating dinner with his family. His younger brother hid his face.

"Oh, do play for us," Mrs. Minting said. "You know so many folk melodies."

"That's right, Nige. Like the woman said, it's your time to shine," Sebastian Minting said definitively.

Looking little happier than Micki, Nigel Minting slunk over to the piano bench. "What do you want me to play?"

"Micks. Tell him," Pauley said cheerfully. "Or I'm picking 'Wannabe' from the immortal album, *Spice*."

"I don't suppose you know 'Lamorna?'" Micki asked Nigel.

He responded by playing a riff from the traditional Cornish air, with such clear skill and verve that his listeners once again broke into applause. Nigel looked up, a smile breaking over his face, and met Jace's eyes across the room. His big brother had steered him true.

"Brilliant. Right. Now, without further ado, I give you Micki Latham and Nigel Minting," Pauley said. "The Storm Veronica Duo."

As Jem reached Rose-Fleur at last, she could hardly focus on the chef de cuisine's latest trick—a flaming onion—for marveling at how swiftly and completely Micki's public singing confidence returned. In a husky voice full of portent, ideal for a dark and stormy night, she sang,

> Twas down in Albert Square,
> I never shall forget,
> Her eyes they shone like diamonds
> And the evening it was wet, wet, wet.
> Her hair hung down in curls,
> She was a charming rover,
> And we rode all night
> In the pale moonlight
> Away down to Lamorna

"The magic is back," Pauley whispered in Jem's ear. "Now I need a glass of wine and five minutes off my aching feet."

"Ms. Jago," Sebastian Minting said, intercepting Jem as she searched for an empty place to sit. "Would you mind sitting with me in that corner? I have a few things to say, and I'd like a bit of privacy."

"Sure," Jem said, casting a longing look Pauley's way before allowing Minting to steer her to one of the outermost two-seaters near the entrance. She hoped fervently that he wanted to talk suspects and clues. If he started thanking her all over again for the insulin, she'd die of mortification.

"First things first," Minting said, seating himself across from Jem. "I don't suppose you've made any progress in finding Beaglehole's killer?"

Jem tried the steak. It tasted better than it smelled, which was really saying something. "Hard to say," she hedged. "I have a prime suspect, but I'm light on proof. Not sure my theory of the case adds up, either. The contestants all turned on each other this afternoon. I'm tempted to pull them into a room and try to kick off another circular firing squad. Then maybe I could decide who merely disliked Lemmy and who seriously wanted him dead."

"Right. Next order of business. It occurred to me just a moment ago that I offered anyone in the hotel who could get Jace insulin ten thousand pounds. You met the moment," Minting said. "Where shall I wire the funds?"

"Not to me," Jem said, astonished.

"You and your friend risked your lives out in the storm. That must be worth something to you."

"It is. It's worth seeing Jace in good health." Jem tucked into the rice. It took all her self-control not to shovel in the entire portion. "Listen, Mr. Minting. If you feel honor-bound to reward someone, I can give you Emily Church's information. But she might feel offended. She told us as a diabetic, she was only too happy to help."

"I don't like feeling indebted," Minting said.

"Neither do I. That reminds me." From her pocket, Jem withdrew the handkerchief with the embroidered initials, **sMa**. "Thanks for that. Sorry I almost kept it."

"I have more than one," he said lightly, fingering the embroidery. "Do you really not know who I am?"

Jem looked up. He wasn't trying to be intimidating. He seemed bemused.

"Only, you're the famous Scilly Sleuth..."

"Yes. Well. You're Sebastian A. Minting from Exeter. You like to read, you have opinions on libraries, and—" Jem broke off suddenly, blinking at him.

"'What light through yonder window breaks?'" he quoted, smiling.

"You're on the board at the Courtney. Sorry. I should have known, but when I worked there, I kept my head down and did my work," she said. "My old boss, Mr. Atherton, dealt with the Powers That Be."

"Indeed he did." Minting tapped the initial **a**. "That stands for Atherton. Lancelot is my cousin."

"Oh. That's... nice," Jem faltered.

"Nice for him, as it got him a situation he desperately wants but can scarcely handle. Not so nice for me. Nepotism cuts both ways, I fear."

Unsure of how to respond, Jem went back to her steak. It was still wonderful, but now she was so gobsmacked by the conversation's turn, she could hardly taste it.

"You know, Lancelot started out as a librarian, but he was too persnickety for the daily slings and arrows. He was cross with his subordinates and unbearable to the buyers. I thought he ought to find another line of work, but the family prevailed upon me to rethink that position," Minting went on. "Because his mother was a great patron of the arts, I had the notion he might do better as an executive. Running interference between the board and our donors, etc., etc. But if I may share an observation in strictest confidence—it's been a massive cock up. We've lost several good people in the last year. Including you."

Jem still didn't know what to say, so she pushed a few grains of rice around her plate. Why hadn't she paused to get some wine on the way to this conversation?

"If I'm being honest," Minting said, "I think perhaps I should sack him and install you in his place."

Jem's jaw dropped. Before she could find any words to reply, someone said, "I'm so sorry to interrupt, Ms. Jago. But could I talk to you?"

"No doubt it can wait a few minutes," Minting said sharply.

Agnetha, already pink-cheeked, blushed deeper. "I know I'm being rude, but it's kind of important. Ms. Jago, if you could just come to Reception, I thought we might talk. About... about what we talked about earlier."

Remembering the hints and hedging from earlier, all of which had culminated in Agnetha fleeing like a spooked gazelle, Jem gave the younger woman an apologetic smile. "I need to finish this conversation first, Agnetha. But the moment I'm done, I'll come and find you at Reception, I promise."

"Right," Agnetha whispered. "I'll be there." She turned and left Kestrel & Peregrine for the second time that night.

"So." Minting sounded like the impatient executive he was. "What do you say?"

"I'm flattered," Jem said truthfully. "Very much so. But I wouldn't feel right about tossing Mr. Atherton out of his job. Not out of any sense of loyalty," she added hastily, lest she seem utterly insincere. "But I think the real reason you're offering this to me is because I went out in the storm for Jace. And while that's lovely, it has nothing to do with me as a professional. Call me bloody-minded, but I want to be recognized for my skills as a librarian, not because I got soaking wet and slipped in the mud."

"Well, we all want professional recognition, I suppose," Minting said mildly. "Even I'm not immune. I have a pet project that's yet to launch, because I have all the big ideas and none of the grinding little specifics. It's a retrospective on Cornwall's long tradition of independence. I call it Cornwall: The Fifth Nation."

For the first time since their discussion began, Jem began to relax. As a Special Collections Librarian, she was always interested in ideas on how to not only preserve history but make it useful and accessible to the public. Minting took the thirty thousand feet view—he wanted school programs, traveling exhibits, an educational programming tie-in with BBC Bitesize, and so on.

"The sky's the limit, really. I know school children receive some rudimentary exposure to their history via small, privately funded schemes," he said. "When you were at school, did you study songs like that?" He nodded toward Micki, who was now singing one of Cornwall's anthems, "Bro Goth agan Tasow."

"We did not," Jem said. "And we learned Chaucer and Milton, but never even heard about A.S.D. Smith, which I think is a crime."

"Then we begin to understand each other," Minting said. "Until Henry VII subdued Cornwall by force, it was practically a nation unto itself. But our region's lack of recognition continues, and the only answer is education..."

They went on like that for some time, batting ideas back and forth about artifacts, literature, and places that suited

Minting's broad framework. With Micki's gorgeous vocals as a backdrop, they talked and talked. The staff, including Xavier, filed out first, and then the hotel guests began to depart. When Rose-Fleur began scrubbing down the teppanyaki grill, Fernsby hurried over to relieve her.

"Go have a proper sit-down," he told her. "Heaven knows you've earned it."

Jem was aware of Pauley and Micki giving her occasional glances. Micki, having finished her set, couldn't stop smiling. Nigel Minting looked pretty pleased with himself, too. Jem knew she should cut off the discussion, but she was genuinely enthralled by Minting's ambition. And because she was a congenital know-it-all, she couldn't resist correcting a few of his misapprehensions about the logistics of such an undertaking. If he really meant to launch Cornwall: The Fifth Nation, he'd need a lot of help.

A shriek came from outside the dining room. Its eerie, echoing quality made the hairs on the back of Jem's neck stand up.

"What on earth?" Minting pushed back his chair.

Another scream came, longer this time. Shooting to her feet, Jem ran toward the sound.

18

GRIM AND GRIMOIRE

No one was screaming inside the corridor, but a few guests stood transfixed, horrified.

"Where?" Jem cried.

A woman pointed to a door near the lifts. "Stairs."

As Jem's hand closed around the handle, the weighty fire door burst open from the other side, knocking her into a group that was hard on her heels. She would've fallen if not for Pauley, who hauled her up. Micki, Fernsby, and Minting also had her back. Looming over her, white-faced and frantic, was Rose-Fleur.

"She's dead," the chef shrieked. "Dead!"

The sight confronting Jem inside the gloomy stairwell was grim. The figure in an ill-fitting business suit lay face down on the cold gray floor. The blow to the head that killed her had dented the back of her skull, mashing her ponytail into the gap. Around her lay bloody fragments of the discarded murder weapon—a massive vase that once sat atop a nearby credenza.

"A dead woman on the floor," Jem said dully. "Her premonition came true."

Behind her, Micki gulped. "I'll get Hack."

"I'll come with you," Pauley said. "Poor Agnetha."

Rose-Fleur burst into tears. "This can't go on. It just can't."

"I know." Fernsby tentatively put an arm around her. She'd lost her toque on the stairs, and her red hair was wild. With a trembling hand, he smoothed it back. "We'll get the mainland police to come. Scotland Yard. The storm can't last forever."

"But it can last the rest of the night," wailed one of the guests in the corridor. "Who'll be next if it lasts all night?"

Jem shivered. Her brainwaves seemed disrupted. She couldn't quite resolve her thoughts into words. But her body did all her thinking for her. She wanted to cry. She wanted to cradle Agnetha's body and beg her forgiveness for putting off a meeting that might have saved her life. And she wanted five minutes alone with the murderer before the authorities took him or her away, hopefully forever.

"We need to secure the scene for the police," Jem heard herself say. Some part of her was still capable of dealing in mundanities, even as the more creative part of her mind struggled to resolve the big picture. "Mr. Minting, will you get us another tablecloth from the ballroom? Once she's decently covered, Mr. Fernsby, I'd like you to lock these stairs so there's no access.

"Rose-Fleur." Jem waited until the weeping woman looked up. "I know this is awful. But please tell me exactly how you found her."

There wasn't much to tell. When Fernsby invited her to take a break, the chef had decided a celebratory ciggie was in order. She'd intended to have a quick one in the stairwell, one of the only places in the hotel without a smoke detector. On entering, she'd discovered Agnetha bloodied on the floor, tried to rouse her, realized she was dead, and screamed.

"Think carefully," Jem urged. "Did you see or hear anything unusual as you approached the door? Someone on their way out? Sounds or voices within?"

Rose-Fleur shook her head. "I can only say this. When I touched her, she was still warm. For a moment, I had hope. I thought she couldn't be dead if she wasn't cold."

"Sounds like you just missed catching the killer in the act," Fernsby said.

"I know." Rose-Fleur burst into fresh tears. "If only I'd come a little sooner..."

"He doesn't mean you might have saved Agnetha. He means you might have been killed, too," Jem said. "Whoever did this was strong and determined. If he couldn't crack you over the head, he probably would've tossed you down the stairs."

"So, we're looking for a male," Minting said, returning with tablecloth in hand.

"Probably," Jem said. "Mr. Fernsby, how much would you say that vase weighed?"

"Nine or ten kilos, I shouldn't wonder."

"Right. So, the killer had to pick it up, carry it through the fire door—probably shifting it to one hand, and then lift it high before bringing it down on Agnetha's head. Striking her hard enough to shatter the vase might have taken more than one blow."

As she spoke aloud, her sleuth's brain weighed her list of suspects against the act.

I never considered Minting or Fernsby suspects, but if I ever had, they're in the clear for this. Rose-Fleur is obviously devastated. I can't see Keir pulling this off without a stepladder. Posh, Isolde, Camille—technically they might have done

it, but that seems about as likely as Mrs. Jones or Mrs.
Morton. That leaves our interlopers, Brown Coat and
Hoodie. Or my last two suspects, Trevor and Xavier. I lean
toward Xavier, if only because he has an acknowledged
history with Agnetha. But I need hard evidence, not a suspi-
cion born when he wouldn't give me a first aid kit.

The lift dinged. Out came Hack, still pale but doing his
best to look official, accompanied by Micki and Pauley.
After being put in the picture, he pulled Jem aside to confer
privately. Then, returning to the group, he began issuing
orders.

"Minting, I'd like you and your sons to go room to room.
Every guest with someplace to go should be on lockdown
for their own safety," Hack said. "Anyone without a place
needs to be assigned. Even a broom closet will do, as long as
the door locks from the inside. Fernsby, I'd like you and
Rose-Fleur to pull the staff together. Would it be possible
for me to interview them in their dormitory? I'd like to sniff
around Agnetha's living space. Who knows what might be
cached there."

"The dormitory is on low ground. Last I looked, it was
flooded," Fernsby said. "Besides, the storm's become more
electrical, don't you think?"

As if to punctuate his point, thunder boomed, and for
the first time, the generator flagged. The lights dimmed,
died for a moment, and came back on. Were they slightly
weaker? Jem couldn't be sure.

"We've already been out there once, before the lightning really started coming," Pauley said. "I wouldn't suggest
pushing your luck."

"What about her locker?" Fernsby suggested.

"Agnetha is the victim, not the perpetrator," Rose-Fleur
said angrily.

"Forgive me, but we don't actually know that," Hack said. "I mean, clearly, she's been murdered, but we don't know what she might have been into before her death." He turned to Fernsby. "Lead on."

"Wait," Micki said. Though still in her borrowed finery, she obviously wasn't ready to lock herself in a room and call it a night. "You passed out assignments to everyone else. What about me and Pauley?"

"You can come with me," Rose-Fleur said. "Make a show of tidying the dining room. Maybe you'll detect something important with the culinary staff."

"Right." Fernsby pushed together the garden lopper's long wooden handles. Its wicked curved maw closed, snapping the steel shank of Agnetha's combination lock in two. As the lock clattered to the floor, Fernsby stepped back, nodding at Hack. "All yours."

"You've done this before," Jem observed. They were in the cloakroom where Jem had borrowed the dog-smelling mac some hours before. Its entryway opened directly onto the service corridor not far from the place Rose-Fleur had taken Pauley, overlooking the flooded courtyard. Jem wished they could close a door for privacy, but at least there was no one about. This part of the hotel seemed deserted.

"Many times, when people forget their combinations, or leave Bay View without taking their belongings."

"Well. Here's a few things to deal with." Hack pulled two notebooks from Agnetha's locker. One, spiral-bound, was girlishly decorated with doodles and stickers. The other, slightly more grown up, was a hardback journal with an owl on the front. After a peek inside each, Hack passed the spiral-bound journal to Jem.

"See if you can figure out what this is, and if it contains anything relevant. This"—he brandished the one with the owl—"seems to be her journal. The first dated entry is from four weeks ago. Is that when she started here?" Hack asked Fernsby.

The manager nodded.

"Right. I saved the final item for you." From the back of the locker, Hack withdrew a Kilner preserving jar half full of something dark and powdery. "This is what we in law enforcement like to call a green, plantlike substance. I need you to keep it safe until forensic backup arrives."

"I'll do one better. I'll take it to Rose-Fleur. She's a genius with herbs and spices. If it's something innocent, like green tea, she'll know right away." Fernsby made as if to depart, but Hack called him back.

"Sorry, but no one should wander about alone. Not even the manager. Cool your heels while Jem and I go through these journals. You're no good to anyone with a vase broken over your skull."

Jem eased down to the floor with her back against the lockers—the same move she'd perfected in her schooldays—and opened Agnetha's spiral-bound notebook. Judging by the fragments of paper clinging to the wires, several pages had been ripped out. The first page was all childish cartoons and words like SHINE and DREAM in block letters. The second page, dated nine years back, declared,

HENCEFORTH THIS BOOKE SHALL BE KNOWN BY THE NAME OF SHADOWS

IN THIS GRIMOIRE
THE WISE WILL FIND
MAGICK ACCORDING TO
THE LAW OF THREE

A grimoire, Jem thought, smiling. *What teen girl didn't have one, or at least want one?*

As she flicked through the pages, she found chants to aid in the passing of maths tests. The putative spells were full of poetical faff—words like "lo" and "o'er"—but were mostly just positive affirmations about the spellcaster's ability to solve trigonometric functions.

The next few pages, CANDLE MAGICK, suggested lighting a blue taper to soothe anxiety, a white taper to encourage optimism, a red taper for romance, and a green candle for money. It was all very Year Seven, and rather endearing, at least to Jem.

"I've got something," Hack said suddenly. "Listen to this:

"'I wasn't terribly chuffed to find Xavier working at Bay View as well. Of course, I didn't march right up to him and ask if he'd put something in King Triton's food and drink to make people sick. I want to say it, but I need a plan first. How can he deny it? Only his favorite customers dodged the bullet. Meanwhile, the people he didn't like wound up puking their guts out. Like me.'"

Turning a few pages, Hack continued.

"'How can he deny it? By just flatly saying he didn't do it. And grinning at me to make sure I know he's lying. Now it's scorched earth between us. He's treating me exactly like he did at St. Mary's School. Making every day hell.'" Hack sighed. "How do you like Xavier for a murder suspect?"

"That brings him a few steps closer," Jem said.

Fernsby sucked in his breath.

"You disagree?" Hack asked him.

"Not necessarily. I don't know what to think." He looked at Jem. "What's in her spiral notebook?"

"Agnetha's grimoire."

"Her what?"

"Spell book. It's one-part Wiccan, one-part generic empowerment, and one-part miserable schoolgirl," Jem said. "The page I'm on now is called, A Rite to Turn Bullies into Friends."

Hack winced. "That's bleak."

"Yeah. And here's the next one: My Signature Blessing Tisane."

"Blessing what?"

"Tisane. It's like an archaic word for tea or elixir. Agnetha's goes like this: one sprig of lemon balm. Four sprigs of fresh mint. One sweet geranium leaf picked by the light of the full moon. And a pinch of ground hemp seed. Hemp was on your allergy list. I wouldn't be surprised if geraniums were, too."

Hack nodded. "I knew it. The second I saw that jar of green stuff, I knew it must have gone into the lemon water."

Fernsby groaned. "That girl. I thought she learned her lesson when she burned the sage. I threatened to sack her on the spot if she ever did anything like that again. So, when you reacted to the water, she must have been too scared to come clean."

"Twice, she tried to talk to me," Jem said. "Maybe she wanted to unburden her conscience, but I don't think so. I think she wanted to accuse someone of poisoning Lemmy."

"Here's another of Agnetha's entries." Hack paged briefly ahead. "The last one, as it happens. From this last week." He read aloud,

"'I need a new job, full stop. Xavier let slip that he knows about the tisane. I don't know when he saw me add it to the water, but he's been aware for some time. I tried to explain that it's purely benign, but he seemed to think it might trigger seasonal allergies or something. He said if someone has a bad reaction, I'd better hope the first aid kit doesn't go missing. If that happens, I might go to prison. He's horrid. I don't know why he has so many devoted customers. I half think he sells drugs as a side hustle. Weed, maybe.'"

"Is that possible?" Jem interrupted, turning to Fernsby.

"Anything is, when you're dealing with a personality like Xavier's," the manager said. "I'll say this, though—he has as many pensioners as friends as people his own age. Runs errands for an old lady who lives on the other side of the island. He told Rose-Fleur she showers him with little gifts. Those *Star Wars* figures at his workstation. His keychain, too."

Jem took that in. She was about to ask a follow-up question when someone standing in the entryway asked cheekily, "Dramatic readings of a dead girl's diary? Really?"

Jem stared at him. She'd first thought him unremarkable, then rather attractive when animated, but now there was something about his face she didn't like. It made her skin crawl.

He spoke calmly, but his hands were trembling. And the faint odor emanating from his pores was one she'd smelled before. Fear.

One glance at Hack told her he'd perceived all of the above about Xavier and possibly more. Putting Agnetha's journal aside, he allowed his right hand to drift in the vicinity of his taser.

"Xavier. Nice of you to turn up." The movement was

subtle, perhaps too subtle for Xavier to notice. "I suppose you've been lurking in the corridor for a while now?"

"I'll never tell." Xavier smirked.

"Answer his questions properly," Fernsby said.

"Or what? You'll sack the best employee you've got? This isn't a real investigation, it's a witch hunt. I know my rights. I can't be questioned without a lawyer present."

"Why did you hate Agnetha?" Jem asked.

"Because she fancied me in school. Embarrassing to have a little freak mooning after me. Worse than that, she followed me here."

"That's no reason to kill her," Hack said.

Xavier scoffed at the accusation. "Are you sure you're all right after sucking down her poisoned water?"

"About that," Jem said. "The ingredients in that preserving jar might put Hack in anaphylaxis, at least in great quantities. But the water in that decanter was pure and clear, without a lot of floaty bits, so I doubt Agnetha put in much. According to her grimoire, it's all about intention. The ritual of blessing the water. But you were absolutely sure someone would drink and be stricken. You even hid the first aid kit to make sure the crisis was as bad as possible."

"What did you add to the water to seal the deal?" Hack demanded.

Xavier forced a chuckle. It sounded hollow. "This is mental. You find a confession in Agnetha's locker, and you turn it around to make me the bad guy?"

Jem took a step toward him. "Xavier. What happened there?" she asked, indicating his right hand. "Cut yourself on a shard?"

He spent less than two seconds contemplating a reply. Then he launched himself down the hallway, faster even than Agnetha had run, hours before.

"Stay here," Jem told Hack, giving him a look to let him know she meant it. The man's police kit probably weighed seven or eight kilograms. He wouldn't get more than a few yards before the wheezing started again.

Xavier's flight took Jem down the same unmarked, identical white corridors that had baffled her earlier. At first, she followed the *thud* of his footfalls, which echoed nicely. Then, just like that, they stopped. One moment Jem was in hot pursuit, and then next, she was at an intersection with no idea which way to turn.

Thinking Fernsby wasn't far behind her, she turned and waited. Just when she was ready to give up—had he stayed behind with Hack?—she heard soft footsteps. Gradually, the Bay View's manager came into view, doing something between a jog and a shamble. Pink with exertion, he was sweating copiously, and his specs were misting over again.

"Not... really... an athlete," he gasped, drawing to a halt.

"Where would Xavier hide?"

Fernsby shook his head. After a moment to fully catch his breath, he added, "Too many places. We'll have to form teams and search systematically. If we do it that way, we'll flush him out. Probably locate the trespassers, too."

"Should we go back for Hack?"

"He said not to. Reminded me he's the only armed person in the hotel. Hopefully. So he'll hold down the cloakroom in case Xavier doubles back."

Fernsby led Jem back to Kestrel & Peregrine's dining room, where the clean-up was completed, and the hotel staff had gathered under Rose-Fleur's direction.

"Safety in numbers," she declared. "Since we can't get to the dormitory, we may all sleep here tonight."

Pauley and Micki greeted Jem with a stereo, "Where's Hack?"

Jem explained everything they'd learned, with the exception of one seemingly incidental detail she kept to herself. Probably, it was nothing. But on the off chance it was everything, she didn't want it disseminated far and wide until she decided how to proceed. She didn't believe Xavier was Lemmy's killer. But she had no doubt he'd murdered Agnetha, and she wanted him caught.

"Xavier?" Rose-Fleur's eyes gleamed. "The little rat. Whatever help you need, just ask."

"I intend on organizing a search party," Fernsby said. "More precisely, a search carried out by several parties simultaneously. We've let this issue of trespassers in the Bay View go on long enough. I want them found as soon as possible."

Pauley sighed. "Rose-Fleur. Is there a PA system?"

Jem regarded her friend curiously. So did Micki, Fernsby, and all the staff, emotionally wrung out and exhausted as they clearly all were. The only person who seemed to know what Pauley was doing was Rose-Fleur.

"Pick up any house phone and dial zero. Your voice will carry throughout the hotel." She added a one-shouldered shrug.

Pauley walked over to the nearest phone and hit a button. Her next words echoed through the dining room and nearby corridor:

"Rhys Tremayne, get your arse to the restaurant. If Pranav's with you, bring him, too."

19

DUMB AND DUMBER ON THE CASE

Pranav Dhillon at least had the grace to look ashamed of himself. He appeared at Kestrel & Peregrine's entryway with his purloined hoodie draped over his arm, the better to return it before taking his punishment. Rhys Tremayne, on the other hand, was Harry Dunne to Pranav's slightly smarter Lloyd Christmas. He strolled into view still wearing his flapping brown coat, the ladies' pink sun hat cocked over one eye. Jem wanted to slap him. But she was too stunned to do anything but listen.

"You know these men?" Fernsby asked Pauley.

"Men may be too strong a word."

"How did you two get to St. Martin's?" Micki asked. "And since when do you know each other?"

Rhys turned expectantly to Pranav, who eyed Pauley nervously.

"The truth is... we met some time ago. When you were visiting me in Penzance, honey bear. Rhys wanted to know more about... er, Felix Catchpole and his helicopter service, so he... that is to say, under the circumstances, and wanting to be discreet in case he'd got it all wrong..."

"I followed you," Rhys told Pauley without a hint of remorse. "Surprise, surprise. Doddering old Felix doesn't exist. But our lad Pranav does exist, and he's been dating you for ages, and *you never said a word*. So, I never said a word, either. I've just been keeping tabs. And when I needed a quick jaunt in the bird to St. Martin's, Pranav was there for me."

"I'm sure this is all very relevant," Fernsby said in chilly tones that would have done Sebastian Minting proud. "But who let you into the Bay View? And how did you obtain those things from my office?"

Rose-Fleur cleared her throat. When Fernsby rounded on her, astonished, she offered an apologetic smile.

"They assured me the situation was desperate. And I couldn't very well turn them back out into the storm."

"But why did they go to you?"

"We once shared a history, ages ago," Rose-Fleur said, accent thickening as she strove to appear mysterious.

"We went out a few times, when the earth was young," Rhys said breezily.

Fernsby eyed Rhys with something akin to dread. Only then did it dawn on Jem that the Bay View's manager was romantically drawn to his chef de cuisine. He was measuring himself against tall, well-muscled, handsome Rhys and seeing all his hopes for Rose-Fleur go up in smoke.

"I still don't understand the disguises," Fernsby said.

Pranav glanced up at Rhys. Then, directing his reply to Pauley, he said, "I understand there was a sort of hiccup. Rhys wanted to drop in on the Bay View and, well, ascertain the lay of the land. He wanted to reconnoiter the situation whilst maintaining—"

"He didn't want me to see him," Jem broke in, finding

herself able to speak at last. "Because I broke up with him this morning."

Rhys made a flowery bow, doffing his floppy pink hat. She slapped it out of his hand.

"Violence is never the answer, Stargazer. And you didn't break up with me. You walked out of the cottage." He grinned. "I admit I was being a *teensy* bit passive-aggressive with all the stuff dumped in the bedroom. I'll say sorry about that—if you'll tell Buck sorry for ruining his morning."

"This hotel has a murderer on the loose," Pauley all but screamed. Rhys stiffened. Pranav looked positively terrified.

"I think you should arrange us into search parties and tell us which parts of the hotel to cover," Rose-Fleur told Fernsby.

"While I appreciate the offer, I think perhaps the searchers should be limited to the... er, larger and more, how shall I put this—"

"Male?" Rose-Fleur interrupted. She turned to address the staffers gathered in Kestrel & Peregrine's dining room. "Which do you prefer, *mes amis*? Sit here together and pray for the dawn, or go and find Xavier while we still can?"

"She's right," Jem said. "We don't have any idea when the storm will break. If it happens in the middle of the night, Xavier could slip out. If he's really lucky, he might nick a boat and get off the island. I'm not saying it's likely, but things haven't exactly gone our way so far. And we owe it to Agnetha to get him in custody." She didn't add her other desire; to see if she could get him to tell all he knew about Lemmy's death. A scenario was taking shape in her mind, but she didn't know how to prove it without Xavier's confession.

Fernsby divided them into three groups. Team One, led

by Rose-Fleur, was made up of half the staff. It was responsible for systematically searching the first floor, including the various large kitchen cabinets, pantries, and staging rooms. Team Two, led by *boulanger* Gregory, comprised the remainder of the staff. It was responsible for systematically searching the top floor. This included knocking on every guest room door and asking the inhabitants if they'd seen Xavier or been asked to shelter him.

Jem told Gregory, "I have reason to believe he might have good relationships with some of the guests. It sounds outlandish that he might get them to hide him, but stranger things have happened."

"So, I reckon that means I'm with you, honey bear," Pranav told Pauley hopefully.

Though Jem suspected her friend was already on the verge of forgiving Pranav, Pauley said sternly, "Mr. Fernsby is in charge of Team Three. It's his call if he wants to put Dumb and Dumber on the case."

Fernsby looked at Jem. "If this man is your boyfriend…" He tailed off on a hopeful note.

"Fine, whatever. Take off that stupid coat," she ordered Rhys somewhat unreasonably.

"He thought you'd recognize the one he wore," Pauley said. "But you didn't, even though it smelled like Buck."

"Sleuth, detect thyself," Rhys said. He raised his hands to ward her off. "Sorry! I did say sorry."

"Right. We're Team Three." Fernsby's gaze took in Jem, Pauley, Micki, Rhys, and Pranav. "We'll head down into the staff and generator areas. At the cloakroom, we'll pick up Sergeant Hackman and see if he has any news. Good luck, everyone."

"One question," Gregory asked. "What do we do if we catch him, or if we need backup?"

"Use the PA," Rose-Fleur said, pointing at a house phone. "Give your location and we'll come running."

At Jem's suggestion, Fernsby unlocked the door beside the lifts and led them past Agnetha's covered corpse. Edging past the vase fragments wasn't easy, and both Micki and Pranav had to gulp and look elsewhere. It was unpleasant, but according to Fernsby, it was the most direct route to the generator room. He had the idea Xavier might be inside it, attempting to sabotage the machine.

"I can't think of another endgame," he told Jem. "If Xavier wants to make a clean getaway, his best bet would be immobilizing the rest of us. That means turning the hotel dark."

"Clever," Jem said.

"Probably impossible," Rhys countered. He insisted on sticking by Jem's side, no matter how she tried to evade or outwalk him. Having his harebrained scheme revealed in front of a roomful of strangers—while wearing a ridiculous disguise, no less—would've chastened most people into silence, but Rhys was nothing if not confident. Movie star looks can do that to you.

"Why impossible?" she asked through her teeth.

"Because Pranav and I were hiding out in there. It's a beast of a machine," Rhys said. "Pretty much enclosed. I mean, if this bloke had some C-4, he might be able to break inside and cause havoc."

"Well, he certainly managed to murder a young woman with the first thing he found to hand," Pauley said stiffly.

They emerged into one of those long white corridors Jem expected to see in her dreams, when and if she finally slept. As Fernsby locked the stairs access door behind them, Rhys said, "You ought to be proud of me, Pauley. I started out with the idea I'd break Pranav's kneecaps.

Maybe crack his skull a bit. But he won me over. And rather than run back to you and wave your Felix Catchpole lie in your face, I decided to let you tell me in your own time."

Pauley looked at Pranav. "Is that true?"

"Mostly. I mean, I'm the one who told Rhys he'd stepped over the line."

"He didn't want to upset her," Rhys stage whispered to Jem. She turned away.

"Let's check out the generator room," she told Fernsby.

They did. While there was ample space for someone to squat, the room was empty apart from the huge gray and red generator, rumbling loudly. Scattered on the floor were three drained plastic soda bottles and a carpet of empty crisp packets.

"I see you left your calling card," Jem told Rhys.

"The fact my cottage doesn't look like that every day is proof enough I love you. Besides, Pranav and I can't live on air. We cleaned out the gift shop and had a feast."

"Feel a bit sick, if I'm being honest," Pranav said.

They continued along the corridor, looking into cul-de-sacs and storage closets. Rhys poked at some ceiling tiles— "That's how they do it on the telly"—but Fernsby assured him there was barely room for a housecat to hide up there, much less a grown man. At the cloakroom, they found Hack waiting for them, taser in hand.

"I haven't seen him," Hack said. "I thought I heard something earlier, but it turned out to be a tree branch hitting that glass door that opens onto the courtyard. Which looks like the end of the world at this point."

"Right." Fernsby sighed. "Let's continue to the loading dock."

Jem and the others followed the manager down another

corridor. It terminated in a pair of automatic doors controlled by a big button on the wall.

"I can't imagine Xavier would choose to be outside, but part of the dock *is* sheltered," Fernsby said, pressing the button. A yellow hazard light flashed overhead as the automatic doors swung slowly outward. As a gust of wind rushed in, he added, "I wouldn't want to hide out near large steel dumpsters in the middle of an electrical storm, but perhaps—"

"Stop!" Hack shouted.

Soaked to the skin, his skin pale and his teeth set, Xavier barreled through the open doors. Jem thought he was heading for Fernsby, but at the last second, he veered toward Hack. The taser deployed, but the electrodes on their long black wires failed to connect. Xavier shoved Hack to the ground, elbowed his way past Micki, who yelped, and took off running.

"Come back here!" Fernsby cried, shaken.

"Are you all right?" Pauley got down beside Hack, who seemed unhurt, only angry.

Spinning on her heel, Jem saw not one but two figures pounding down the corridor. Xavier was in the lead, but long-legged Rhys was closing the gap. Of course he was—he ran two miles every morning.

She gave chase. It seemed likely that Xavier might try to access the stairs, or perhaps barricade himself in the generator room. But to her surprise, he made for the glass vestibule facing the courtyard. Flinging open the door, he dashed into the courtyard. Rhys barreled out after him.

"Rhys!"

Xavier shot across the courtyard, leaping over storm debris in his effort to evade Rhys. He seemed determined to reach the staff dormitory, despite the moat of runoff around it. He was halfway there when a massive bolt of lightning struck, impaling him between earth and sky.

"*Rhys!*"

Jem flung herself through the glass door, running blindly into the night. Rain battered her face; the sheer power of the wind driving itself into her pummeled her to a standstill. Then someone seized her around the waist from behind and dragged her, twisting and kicking like a wild animal, back inside again.

"Stop fighting," Hack said in her ear. "You can't save him by going out there."

"I have to get to Rhys," she wailed. She didn't recognize her own voice. It seemed to belong to someone else.

"Jemmie, he's okay. It's all right. *He's okay.*" Suddenly Pauley was in front of her, also wet from head to toe, though only from the gusts of rain sweeping into the corridor. "Look!"

Jem could barely see what Pauley was trying to show her. So many transitions, from fluorescent bulbs to inky blackness to overhead glare again, had dazzled Jem's eyes, making fine details blur. Slowly, she made out two figures running toward them. No—just one figure who was carrying the other. Jem couldn't focus on his face, but her heart leapt all the same. Between Rhys and Xavier, only Rhys had the strength to toss a grown man over his shoulder like a sack of flour and bear him to safety.

"He got hit right in front of me." Rhys lowered Xavier to the floor. As Pauley pulled the glass door closed, grunting with the effort of shutting out the storm, Hack released his grip on Jem. She stumbled toward Rhys and Xavier, turning an ankle in her haste.

"You could have been killed," she shrieked at Rhys, picking herself up angrily. "You could have *died!*"

Wild-eyed, his hair plastered to his skull and his clothes soaked right through, Rhys stared at her with obvious incomprehension.

"Sorry," he shouted. "Can't hear. Ears ringing from the thunder." Panting, he dropped to his knees beside Xavier.

"Is he breathing?" he shouted. "I don't think he's breathing."

"Let me see." Hack knelt to examine Xavier as he'd knelt to look over Lemmy Beaglehole, ten hours and a lifetime ago.

Xavier's eyes were open. His mouth was open, too, in a permanent look of astonishment. He'd run into the storm coatless, clad only in his Bay View uniform: black button-down shirt, black trousers, socks, and shoes. Now his feet were bare and white, the toes marked with a strange branching design. The stink of burned flesh made Jem gag, but she steeled herself to look at the man.

How hot is a lightning bolt? Her librarian's brain delved within its deep stacks, searching through books she'd devoured over a lifetime of reading. *30,000 degrees Kelvin. Hotter than the surface of the sun.*

If that was true, it seemed like Xavier should have been incinerated outright. But while his singed hair and eyebrows suggested electrocution, only a spot in the vicinity of his left hip pocket had actually combusted. The finger of blue-white electricity had touched him there, overloading his heart and brain on its inexorable journey from heaven to the earth.

"No respiration," Hack said.

Micki and Pranav hung back, watching mutely as Fernsby said into the receiver of a wall-mounted house phone, "Search is over. Gather in Decant Resist and the common area for further instructions. Repeat, search is over."

He paused to look at Jem. "Should I announce the danger is over, too?"

She shook her head.

"We should try resuscitation," Hack told Rhys. "I'll breathe for him. You do the chest compressions." He had to repeat himself twice for Rhys to understand, but once they got started, they made a heroic stab at reviving Xavier. As a police officer, Hack was well-versed in lifesaving techniques, and Rhys had been CPR-certified since his surfing days. They worked on Xavier long past any real hope of revival, giving up only after several pauses to check for a response.

"His pupils are blown. He's gone," Hack said, sitting back on his heels and regarding the body angrily. "Damn it, I wanted him to live. I'm sure he killed Agnetha, but why?"

"I wonder what he had in his pocket." Rhys no longer shouted, but he still spoke far louder than necessary. "Coins, maybe?"

"It's not like we have to preserve the body forensically. We know what killed him," Hack said. "Might as well dig in and find out."

He pushed aside the blackened fabric, which crumbled to flakes like chimney soot. On Xavier's pale chest, a livid red design bloomed and branched like a hellish vine. It reminded Jem of patient education diagrams depicting a cluster of nerves as delicate curling brushstrokes.

Lichtenberg figure, her librarian's brain supplied. *Hallmark of a lightning strike on the human body.*

With a grunt of disgust, Hack held up something with soot-stained fingers. "A key."

"What's that stuck to it?" Jem asked.

"Um... remains of a keychain, I think. Some kind of novelty craft thing."

"Let me see it," Jem said, leaning closer to inspect the yarn fragments.

"That key got really hot, huh?" Pauley said, pointing at Xavier's exposed hip. "Look at that."

What Jem had taken for part of the Lichtenberg figure was, upon closer examination, the purple outline of the key. Had Xavier survived the strike, his Lichtenberg figures would have faded in time, but a scar in the shape of a key would have remained for the rest of his days.

Hack pulled a clear evidence bag from his duty belt and dropped the key and keychain fragments inside. "Not sure if it will turn out to be evidence of anything, but a man can dream."

Rhys tapped his left ear. "God, I hope I don't wind up with tinnitus for life. That thunderclap after the lightning strike went off like a bomb blast in my head." He rounded on Jem, nostrils flaring. "As for you—don't ever run out into a storm like that again. You risk your life too much as it is. Don't start courting death just for the thrill of it."

This was so monumentally thick-headed and nonsensical, Jem emitted a strangled scream. Hack placed a steadying hand on her shoulder.

"Remember. Murder isn't legal."

"Time out," Pauley said. "We can all turn on each other once the storm ends. I can't walk around like this—like I went swimming in my clothes. Jemmie, you're soaked, too. Let's go up to the room and change."

"Hey. You know who else is soaked? Me," Rhys said.

"So sad," Pauley said. "Maybe Mr. Fernsby will let you towel off in the employees' lavatory if you ask him nicely. Coming, Jem?"

"I think we should all go up together. Not because you deserve to be included," she told Rhys, who'd just shot Pauley a triumphant grin, "but because I think I know who killed Lemmy. Now I just have to work out a way to prove it."

20

DEVIL'S IN THE DETAILS

The garden-view room for two no longer seemed terribly luxurious with six people using it all at once.

Hack, Pranav, and Micki, all dry, took time to get acquainted. Jem and Pauley, who'd hoped to change back into their first set of clothes, found them still quite damp. The Bay View-provided hair dryer, which was very low wattage, did little to alleviate the situation, so they decided to change into the only dry clothes they had left—pajamas.

"What do you think?" Jem asked, emerging from the bathroom in an old library festival T-shirt emblazoned with *I Read Banned Books* and plaid pajama bottoms.

Rhys answered with a wolf whistle. She scowled.

"I meant, am I decent enough for public consumption?"

"I think so," Pranav said.

"It's half one. I don't think anyone will complain," Hack said. "Rhys is the one who'll raise eyebrows. He chucked his shirt in the bin."

"It smelled like burnt... something," Rhys said, clearly meaning burnt Xavier. "I kept the jeans even though they're damp. What's wrong with shirtless?" He spread his arms in a seemingly self-deprecating way—one that just happened to show off his well-defined pecs, delts, and triceps—and grinned cheekily.

"Put your coat on," Pauley said, emerging from the bathroom in her black goth onesie. The yellowish skull-and-crossbones motif glowed in the dark. "We want people paying attention to what Jem and Hack have to say, not goggling over you."

"I like those pjs," Pranav said. "When the lights go out again, I'll know just where you are."

"Think that's likely?" Rhys asked, reluctantly getting into his horrible, dog-scented mac, which he declined to button up. Without a shirt beneath it, he looked like a party stripper in stage one of the big reveal.

"Lights always go out after the sleuth gets all the suspects in one room," Pranav said. "How can you not know that?"

"Well, in that kind of murder mystery, there's usually a corpse when the lights come back on, but I think we're past that now," Jem said. "Our killer wants to wrap this up and go home. Lemmy was the only planned death. Agnetha and Xavier happened when things went off-script."

Pranav nodded uncertainly. Then began in a diffident tone, "I hope you don't take this the wrong way, but..."

"But my theory's hard to believe?" Jem smiled at him. Hack, Pauley, and Rhys felt the same, though they'd been too loyal to say so outright. And whatever reservations they felt about her conclusion, they'd all agreed to go along with this public confrontation. Even Hack, who was putting his professional reputation on the line by allowing her to stage an ambush that might blow up in both their faces. His trust meant a lot to her.

He's a wonderful friend. In another life, we might have

made a good couple, Jem thought. Her gaze shifted to big, blond Rhys in all his strapping, stripperish glory. *Except I've been in love with one man my whole life, and somehow, we'll find a way to make it work. It's the only way we'll ever be happy.*

Someone rapped at the door. Pauley let Fernsby in. The manager looked grimly satisfied, as if he'd won some sort of battle.

"They're all downstairs. All of them. A few of the guests got shirty, but Sebastian Minting cut them down to size. He's a good man to have on your side." Fernsby looked at Jem. "That's down to you."

She shrugged. Best not to take too much credit for Minting's change of heart until she found out whether his talk of a new library job materialized—as she desperately hoped it would.

"So, no one tried to weasel out of it? Really?"

"Well, Mrs. Ellery said she didn't think the proceedings would be appropriate for her children. I asked one of the cooks to babysit the kiddies with fairy plasters and coloring books from the gift shop, and that did the trick. So, Mrs. Ellery and her husband agreed to come down. They seemed rather relieved if you ask me. I promised to check lost-and-found on my way down and fetch that Barbie from the box."

"Let's go, then," Jem said. "Maybe it will have a shirt that fits Rhys."

Downstairs, Decant Resist was filled to capacity, with the spillover taking up the common room. Some of the guests looked sleepy or wrung out from the long night—it was going on two a.m.—but most were surprisingly perky.

Someone had even taken it upon themselves to uncork a few bottles of red wine, serving it up in plastic cups from the now-defunct water station.

The wine must have been doing its work. Someone shouted, "Huzzah!" as Jem, Hack, Fernsby, and the others arrived.

"They're having a regular piss-up," Micki murmured in Jem's ear.

"Can you blame them? Three dead, and the storm's still raging," Jem replied.

Sebastian, Jace, and Nigel Minting seemed to have appointed themselves the unofficial shepherds of the guest contingent. They'd stationed themselves at a spot where common area travertine tiles became dark carpet, marking Decant Resist's territory. When Minting Snr.'s eyes met Jem's, he gave her a tight smile. No outbursts or violence would go unchallenged on his watch.

The Bake Off contestants had grouped themselves together in the common area. Mrs. Jones and Mrs. Morton shared a sofa with Isolde; Trevor hovered behind them, hands jammed into his pockets, swaying nervously. His expression was stoic, but perhaps that was easier with his hair completely obscuring his eyes.

Camille sat on a club chair with a lined yellow pad and pen in her lap. She'd dressed up for this late-night occasion, with full makeup, dangly earrings, and a bow in her pink hair. The smile she gave Jem faded slightly when she saw Jem's PJ's and Pauley's glow-in-the-dark skulls and crossbones.

"Goodness. Did Mr. Fernsby drag you out of bed? I thought this meeting was your idea."

"It was. Xavier ran out into the storm, but he wasn't the only one who got drenched. This was all I had left to wear."

Jem indicated Camille's yellow pad. "Will you be taking minutes?"

"No, I've been working on the case," Camille said eagerly. "Doing my own investigation. You're not the only one with a keen eye for the truth."

"I notice two suspects are still following you around, Ms. Jago," Keir said. "Pauley Gwyn served the fatal cake. Micki Latham was a humble contestant, just like the rest of us." He tried to make the accusations sound like friendly banter, but there was real animosity in his eyes. "Did you exonerate your ragtag gang of accomplices purely on the basis of friendship?"

"Keir," Posh murmured. She looked exhausted.

"I'm just saying what everyone's thinking. Then again, maybe I'm being too harsh. I thought this was meant to be a Miss Marple-style confrontation. But apparently, it's a knitting class."

"This isn't for me." Approaching Mrs. Morton, Jem offered the old lady the skein of yarn from Fernsby's lost-and-found box. "You said something about liking to keep your hands busy."

"Yes, indeed. Thank you, love." Beaming up at Jem, Mrs. Morton accepted the royal-blue yarn and crochet hook. "I'm a fair knitter but a terrific crocheter."

"You'd better hope the storm ends soon," Mrs. Jones told Fernsby. "Otherwise, Vera will have this hotel covered in doilies and antimacassars in nothing flat."

Unlike her friend, who seemed bright-eyed and content to be there, Mrs. Jones looked like a woman in need of sleep. All the impishness and charm Jem recalled from that morning seemed to have fled. Isolde still looked quietly miserable, as she had when she'd confessed the killer dessert was hers.

Rhys, now decently covered up thanks to an XXL shirt he'd found in the gift shop, sat down with Pranav on the common area's remaining seats. Hack stationed himself between the group and the lifts. Fernsby, Rose-Fleur, and Gregory joined him.

"All right, Jem Jago." Rose-Fleur Frenchified every syllable, perhaps to make up for all the moments she'd accidentally dropped the accent during the night's tumultuous events. "Everyone knows Xavier died, and how. What else can you tell us?"

Camille's hand shot up like Hermione Granger's.

"Um... yes?" Jem asked, calling on her reluctantly.

"Do we have witnesses who can verify Xavier was killed by a lightning strike?"

"I saw it happen," Rhys said.

"You actually saw the bolt touch his body?" Camille sounded skeptical.

"I was so close, I came away smelling flambéed. Had to bin my shirt." He gestured to his yellow BEACHES BE CRAZY T-shirt. "You can't think I'm wearing this on purpose?"

"All right." Camille jotted something on her yellow pad. "Only, we have a person behaving in a very suspicious manner, and before we can question him, he turns up dead. Terribly convenient, don't you think?"

Jem looked at Hack, who bit his lip to hide a smile. Was this what it felt like to have an interloper breaking in with theories all the time?

"Let's start at the beginning," Jem said. "This afternoon, about two hours before the contest started, Sergeant Hackman served himself a cup of water from this area. He had what turned out to be a severe allergic reaction to—"

"Jem, if you know who killed Beaglehole, just tells us.

Don't natter on endlessly in the middle of the night," Mrs. Jones snapped.

"I know it's late," Jem said calmly. "But if I just blurt out my conclusions, you won't accept it. You'll bombard me with a hundred questions and we'll be here all night. Just let me say my piece. Then you can all decide if it has merit."

Mrs. Jones pursed her lips. "Sounds like you have no evidence."

Camille's hand shot up.

"Camille, put your hand down. Mrs. Jones, why would you say that? Even in a trial, lawyers submit their opening arguments before they trot out the exhibits."

"This isn't a trial. It isn't even an arrest, from what I can gather." Mrs. Jones turned to regard Hack. "Well, Mr. Policeman? Is there any evidence? Because if not, I don't have time for this, and neither does Isolde. She's had a perfectly dreadful day and being dragged down here is the absolute limit. The rest of you lot might not care to sleep, but peace and quiet suits us fine."

"It's all right, Gran," Isolde said.

"No, it isn't. And they can't keep us here." Mrs. Jones rose, gesturing for Isolde to do the same.

"Low blood sugar," Mrs. Morton said, her eyes on her crochet needle. It was already bobbing and weaving, turning a single blue strand into a clump of possibility. "Find one of those kiddies. Maybe they can spare her a chocolate bar or a ring pop."

"Jem can't keep you here, but I can," Hack said. "Sit down."

Mrs. Jones stared at him. "What are you going to do? Taser a pensioner?"

"Do it," Keir said. "The islanders will issue you a commendation. Pin a medal on your chest."

"Don't you have some valuable possessions to gamble away?" Mrs. Jones said acidly.

Handcuffs at the ready, Hack took a single deliberate step toward her. "Earlier, you were pleading with me to chain you to a credenza. I'll do it now if you don't sit down and listen quietly."

Mrs. Jones glared at Hack for so long, Jem thought she might actually choose to test his resolve. In the end, however, she sat back down with a huff of fury.

"Right. Starting over," Jem said. "Regarding Sergeant Hackman's allergic reaction. Something in the water put him in anaphylactic shock. For a while, we considered that the first case of poisoning. But it wasn't. Not deliberately, anyway. We learned this after Agnetha was found dead. Mr. Fernsby opened up her locker and Sergeant Hackman took a quick look through her belongings, searching for clues as to who might have killed her and why. He found a journal that mentioned several pertinent facts—"

"Such as, she used to visit King Triton's quite often," Camille cut in. Apparently, she'd decided that if raising her hand like the cleverest witch at Hogwarts wouldn't work, she'd just shout answers out. "If memory serves, Agnetha got so sick, she had to go to hospital. When she got hired on here and found Xavier on staff, she might have asked him what he knew. *Or* suspected him of being the culprit."

"Well, actually, yes," Jem said, irritated by the necessity of agreeing with Camille.

"I don't understand," Posh said.

"That's because we've made a few leaps ahead," Jem said. She explained about Agnetha's grimoire, her blessing tisane, and Xavier's warning that a guest might react poorly. "We'll never know if Agnetha's herbs alone affected Hack, or if Xavier added a little something extra. Because he hid the first aid kit, I think he did."

"I'm so glad my civil liberties were trampled so I could learn all about New Age hoo-hah and spiteful twenty-some-things," Mrs. Jones said.

"Low blood sugar," Mrs. Morton repeated softly. Her clump of yarn was now a neatly defined square, growing by the second into a rectangle.

"Mrs. Jones, I should inform you, I've moved you from my Likely Suspects column to my Prime Suspects column," Camille said. "You're behaving like someone who hears the clock ticking and is desperate for a distraction."

"Young lady. Unlike you, I didn't blow into the islands three years ago. I've lived my whole life in the Isles of Scilly. And this entire community will vouch for me. Apart from the occasional reprobate," Mrs. Jones added, looking at Keir.

"Oh, I know you're part of the island mafia," Camille replied. "Even if I didn't, the way you behaved in the lobby, screeching over Lemmy Beaglehole—only someone who thinks she's untouchable acts that way."

"What's the island mafia?" Micki asked.

"Ex-council members who have been here so long, they still try to run everything," Pauley replied. "People used to say my mum was part of the island mafia. She laughed and said if that was true, there'd be a lot more people sleeping with the fishes."

"When Lemmy Beaglehole was named judge, no one was happy about it," Camille continued. "We all knew he'd take us to the woodshed whether we deserved it or not. I almost pulled out. I know for a fact that Posh had a melt-down, because everything Keir makes tastes like Styrofoam. But not Mrs. Jones."

Turning in her seat, Camille looked the old lady in the

eye. "She rang up the council. She talked to Lemmy's boss at *All Things Penzance*. I think she probably even tried to twist Mr. Fernsby's arm. I was asking around with the staff, and they've seen Mrs. Jones here several times in the last month. The rest of the little coterie, too. Trevor and Isolde and Mrs. Morton. But most often, it was Mrs. Jones."

That was actually salient information, even if it came via Camille. Jem turned to address the Bay View's staffers. "Is that true?"

"I saw Mrs. Jones last Tuesday," one volunteered.

"I saw her yesterday."

"I think she was here last week, but I can't swear to it."

Trevor bestirred himself for the first time. "I never set foot in this place until today. I mean, yesterday."

Isolde said, "Of course, Gran and I are here frequently. We live half a mile away and we've just opened a new shop. If I want the residents of St. Martin's to support my business, I have to support theirs. That means popping in here for a quick one or nibbles at the café."

"I've borrowed one of the hotel golf carts to run my errands," Mrs. Morton said, eyes still on her crocheting. "Sometimes I come for it myself. Sometimes I pay a boy to fetch it round to my cottage."

"I don't know about you, Jem Jago," Camille said. "But I'm ready to say right now that our killer is Mrs. Jones. She had the motive. And she had the opportunity since she would have been nearby when her granddaughter baked her cake."

This accusation gave way to a miniature uproar. Minting shushed the guests who were high-fiving and clinking wineglasses, as if their personal favorite had won the race. Keir and Posh seemed pleasantly surprised, but most of the other suspects looked unimpressed by Camille's theorizing.

"Right. So, tell us, Camille," Jem said. "Did Mrs. Jones kill Agnetha, too?"

"Yes," Camille said stoutly. "I just haven't worked out the details."

"The devil's in the details, I think you'll find," Jem said. "Speaking of details, Isolde, do you recognize this?" She passed over her mobile for the other woman to examine. Onscreen was the photo she'd snapped in Cake Me Proud— the dusty mauve envelope Keir claimed to have found lying rather obviously in a rubbish bin.

"Yes, it's one of mine. Where did you find it?"

"In your kitchen. It's a long story. But you left the door unlocked again. And you should know the envelope smells of almonds. Which probably indicates cyanide."

21

STITCHED UP

"Cyanide?" Isolde looked as if she might faint. "Why were you in my kitchen?"

"Pauley and I went out in the storm looking for something important," Jem said. "We stopped by Cake Me Proud to shelter under the porch and saw a light inside. Keir's lantern, as it turns out."

"You broke into my place?" Isolde stared at Keir.

"The door was unlocked. And you admit you baked the fatal cake," he said. "I thought I'd have a look around. It's not as if Hackman was fit to do it. And when Jem turned up, I showed her what I found. The envelope that once contained powdered cyanide. Your envelope, matching the stationery in your desk."

Isolde gasped. "You were in my *bedroom*?"

Whatever comeback Keir planned was lost as Trevor's hands closed around the little man's throat. One minute, the miniature silver fox was happily hurling accusations at Isolde. The next, he was being throttled by a man who'd finally pushed the hair out of his eyes.

"Stop! Let him go, or I'll taser you!" Hack thundered.

It took a policeman, three Mintings, a hotel manager, and a dude in a BEACHES BE CRAZY T-shirt to pull Trevor off Keir. The little man was left red-faced and panting, but not seriously injured, as Trevor was cuffed and made to sit across the room.

"I'm sorry," Trevor said meekly. "I just couldn't let him treat my wife that way."

Isolde looked at him with shining eyes. "Thanks, Trev."

"You're welcome," he said softly.

Isolde rounded on Keir. "You still haven't told me why you were in my bedroom?"

"Leave him alone. Can't you see he's unwell?" Posh cried.

"I think his throat will be sore for a while, but I think I can answer that," Jem said.

"So can I," Camille said. "To plant evidence."

"No. It was because he really hoped Isolde was guilty. Think about what happened at King Triton's. It was a popular little crab shack until so many people got sick," Jem said. "Agnetha had a theory that Xavier was the culprit, which seems highly likely. But why? Was it pure malice? Or was there another reason?"

She turned to Mrs. Jones.

"That story you told me about helping Isolde open her own bakery. Convenient that a property came open on St. Martin's just when you needed it, isn't it? What are the odds?"

Mrs. Jones said nothing.

"There's plenty of bad blood between you and Keir. That was obvious from this afternoon on," Jem continued. "I can't prove it, but I think he put two and two together, just like me. You're part of the island mafia. You know everyone in the islands, including Xavier. You must have made it worth his while to shut down King Triton's so you could swoop in and claim it for Isolde."

Isolde stared at her grandmother. "That... that's not true, is it?"

"Of course not." Mrs. Jones looked away.

"It's true," Keir said hoarsely. "Xavier all but admitted it to me. That old bat paid him to make King Triton's clientele go away."

Mrs. Jones waved a hand. "All's fair in love and business. Besides, I admit nothing."

"Right. So. We know that Keir says he found an incriminating piece of evidence lying in plain sight, just waiting to be discovered, in Isolde's bakery," Jem continued. "And I might as well tell you, I don't believe for a minute that Isolde would have poisoned her own cake in some kind of weird double-bluff. From the first, she thought she'd been stitched up, and I agree with her.

"So, let's go back to this morning, Isolde. When you came to Bay View to get your gran off the lobby floor, you said you'd just finished your cake. Do I have that right?"

Isolde nodded.

"You said that you might have left your shop unlocked. Did you?"

"Yes."

"Did you see any evidence that someone had been inside Cake Me Proud while you were called away?"

"No."

"Was your cake already boxed up?"

"No. It was sitting on the countertop. But it was fully decorated," Isolde said. "I don't see how anyone could have poisoned it in a way that would have killed Lemmy so quickly. Sprinkling a little cyanide on top wouldn't make him keel over like that."

"When did you decide on the design for your cake?" Jem asked.

"Tuesday night."

"Tell me how it went."

"Well, Gran and I always meet Trev and Mrs. M. for supper on Tuesdays. We had a nice meal together and sketched out our designs. We wanted to tell each other everything so there was no chance anyone accidentally did something similar. Two similar cakes would probably cancel each other out in the judging."

"Is that likely? Different bakers somehow coming up with the same design?"

"Probably not among bakers who don't know each other. But we've known one another forever," Isolde said. "Trev and I trained at the same institute. Plus, we think alike when it comes to cakes," she added, shooting him another smile. "And besides, we help each other. Give each other tips and little notes on how to improve our entry. Between the three of us, we reckoned one of us had a good shot of winning."

Jem let that hang in the air for a moment. Not because it was especially important or surprising, but because she was searching for signs of anxiety in one certain person—and finding none at all. Either her designated prime suspect was innocent, or as cool under fire as those corpses in the freezer.

"Mrs. Jones," Jem said at last. "You told me you staged that one-woman protest in the lobby to try and get Lemmy sacked. But that wasn't true, was it?"

"What else would it be?"

"I think someone asked you to get Isolde away from Cake Me Proud. It was a last-minute request. You had to think up something so outrageous, and so unreasonable, that

Mr. Fernsby would ring Isolde and tell her to rush over to the Bay View."

"But that's absurd," Isolde said. "If Gran wanted me, she could've just rung me herself."

"That would have defeated the purpose," Jem said. "It had to seem like your grandmother was pitching a wally. You were pretty frustrated when you arrived. I'll bet when you got home, you were in a hurry to change clothes, box up the cake, and get back for the contest. And you never noticed that the cake you baked had been swapped with a lookalike. Or that incriminating evidence had been left in your bin. Evidence meant for the police to find—except the storm hit, and Keir found it instead."

Mrs. Jones blinked at Jem. Then she turned slowly to regard her dear friend of fifty-five years, Mrs. Vera Lynn Morton, who was still crocheting, her lips crooked in an amiable half-smile. In a vicious whisper, Mrs. Jones asked, "What have you done?"

"Nothing anyone can prove, from the sound of it," Mrs. Morton said, not bothering to look up.

22

CAT'S PAWS

An excited susurration rippled through the guests, like a wind bending dry grass. It was the spontaneous utterance Jem had hoped for. But it wasn't enough. The community and the law would expect more evidence—much more.

"You told me Trevor wrote Isolde a letter expressing his true feelings," Mrs. Jones said to Mrs. Morton. "You said he was wavering on whether or not to give it to her. And if I created a big enough stink, you could pluck it from his overnight bag and tuck it somewhere in Isolde's kitchen for her to find. It was all in service of getting them back together."

Mrs. Morton went right on crocheting. Mrs. Jones addressed her former grandson-in-law.

"Trevor, did you write Isolde a letter?"

He shook his head.

"But you wanted to, didn't you?" Jem said, unable to resist helping him out. "The fact you would even enter this contest to be near Isolde was a very brave act, in my opinion. Mrs. Jones told me all about the lovely little bakery you had in Penzance. Until Lemmy came along with one of his viral takedowns. He insinuated that your place wasn't clean. That your food might make people sick. It was unbelievably cruel, but that was Lemmy's stock-in-trade. And it had a profound effect on you, didn't it?"

Trevor frowned, his eyes darting helplessly as he seemed to struggle for words. Isolde spoke up instead.

"He shut down. Turned into a shell of himself. I don't know how much of that was losing his business, and how much of it was—" She broke off, regarding her ex-husband with a dawning new tenderness. "And how much was dealing with me, completely full of myself, back from the institute and ready to conquer the world. I wasn't the best wife."

"I wasn't bothered," Trevor said softly.

"You gave up on him," Mrs. Morton said. She was still crocheting at a fast clip. Nothing in the proceedings thus far had caused her concentration to lapse or her fingers to falter. "He needed you and you filed for divorce. He's a dead man now, except he's still walking around. But he wouldn't hear a single word against you. Insisted we carry on, the four of us, as if everything was still pitch perfect. I didn't want them back together. I wanted her out of his life for good."

Camille cleared her throat. "Jem, I think I speak for everyone when I say, I'm confused. Are you really accusing poor old Mrs. Morton of killing Lemmy?"

Jem turned to Mrs. Morton. "Would you care to answer that?"

"No," she replied serenely. In less than half an hour, she'd turned out several inches of what looked like a jumper sleeve, or perhaps a slender muffler. "I'm waiting for you to tell me everything you think I've done."

"Fine. I think this all started when Mrs. Jones hired

Xavier to give King Triton's a reputation for food poisoning," Jem said. "Maybe he came up with an additive that was guaranteed to make people violently ill. Maybe Mrs. Jones did. Anyone with an internet connection and a willingness to experiment can brew up an emetic.

"Once Isolde opened Cake Me Proud, I think your resentment grew and grew, Mrs. Morton. Trevor had lost his business and his marriage, but Isolde was thriving. So, you approached Xavier on your own. According to his reputation, he was all about the money. You could have paid him enough to start brewing something stronger than emetics. And again, with an internet connection, it's not hard to find a recipe for cyanide."

"Still haven't heard any proof," Mrs. Morton said.

"I found apple pips simmering in my kitchen," Rose-Fleur said. "And a bushel of peaches was tossed out, except for the pits. Either of those can be used to make a toxic decoction."

"Xavier was always in and out of the kitchen behind your back," Gregory put in. "I warned him off several times."

"Registered a complaint with me about it," Fernsby added.

"By the time the Bake Off rolled around, Xavier had supplied you with the cyanide," Jem said. "Because you knew exactly what Isolde's cake would look like, you made a poisoned duplicate. Probably you thought there'd be ample time to make the switch. But there wasn't, so you duped your friend of however many decades into creating a fuss, so you could stitch up her granddaughter."

"But what about—" Camille began.

"Let me finish. I don't think Agnetha was meant to die. She was locked in her own little war with Xavier. He bullied her in school, and he bullied her here. Even stole her bead box. And when he saw her putting that blessed tisane into the water decanter, he didn't go to Mr. Fernsby. He wanted something terrible to happen, and it almost did. That got Agnetha to look at him more critically and put two and two together. She never mustered the courage to come right out and say it, but I'm sure she thought Xavier was the Mad Poisoner. That he somehow poisoned a cake for kicks. And when she confronted him, he killed her. My only question is," Jem said more pointedly, "did he do that on his own, or did you put him up to it, Mrs. Morton?"

"You have nothing to tie me to that young man," Mrs. Morton said.

"I believe we have one thing," Hack said. He held up the clear plastic evidence bag containing the metal house key found on Xavier's body. Attached to it was a half-incinerated crocheted keychain.

"That's one of your sunflower designs, isn't t?" Jem asked. "I recognized it from last week. When you sold sweets and tchotchkes at Bart's pirate festival."

"Yes, indeed." Winking at Jem, Mrs. Morton held out the half-completed muffler. "Proof at last. I've spent all evening hoping for a demonstration of your skills. And didn't I play my part perfectly?"

Jem was momentarily dumbstruck. Fortunately, her curiosity restored her voice.

"Did you tell Xavier to kill Agnetha?"

"Good Lord, no. She had no proof and no credibility. She might have made a little trouble for him, but not for me. I told him to charm her. Give her a roll in the hay. He's the one who decided to shut her up for good." She shook her head. "Excitable boy. Not the best cat's paw."

"What?" Jem asked.

"Cat's paw. You know. The useful idiot who takes all the chances at the mastermind's behest. I'm the mastermind," Mrs. Morton said comfortably. "And I was beginning to worry that this whole thing would fizzle out with Sergeant Hackman just throwing up his hands. That one's all looks and no substance, if you ask me."

"Have you finally gone round the bend?" Mrs. Jones shouted. "You murdered Beaglehole. And you lied to get my help."

"Cat's paw number two," Mrs. Morton said. "Jem, darling, you were so eager to nail me, I think you skipped a detail. That envelope Keir found in the bin wasn't really a cyanide vessel. Xavier's decoction was liquid. But I was afraid the thickie police would miss an unlabeled bottle, so I nicked one of Isolde's envelopes and sprinkled it with almond extract. Just enough to be sure no one could miss the connection."

"I can't believe this. You really intended to fit up my Isolde for murder?" Mrs. Jones asked.

"She was sure to get off in the end." Mrs. Morton shrugged. "You know the courts these days. But it would have jerked a knot in her pretty mane, now, wouldn't it? Oh, close your mouth, Lobelia. If I'd really wanted to get even, I could have poisoned her plate at our weekly Tuesday night supper. Watched her go face first into the boiled potatoes."

"Gran!" Trevor cried, aghast.

"But that would have been too simple. When you're a mastermind, you make things complicated. You choose your cat's paws. You devise a complicated method for murder. You lay a trap for the patsy to take the fall. You even add in a few hints to make it sporting," she added, turning back to Jem. "At first, I thought I'd gone overboard with all of my hints. But only the most obvious one—Xavier's keychain—caught your eye."

"What are the other hints?" Jem asked.

"I'll show you."

Rising, Mrs. Morton made for Decant Resist's darkened bar. Grown men stepped back to avoid her, as if a septuagenarian who weighed perhaps seven and a half stone soaking wet might kill them where they stood.

"Shouldn't you handcuff her?" Camille demanded of Hack.

"I kind of want to see what she's talking about," Hack said.

"Here's one!" Mrs. Morton called, plucking one of the little *Star Wars* figures from beside Xavier's cash register. "I made these for Xavier to display. The art form is called amigurumi. This is Baby Yoda. Isn't he cute? And this one is the Mandalorian."

"I noticed them," Jem groaned. "And I knew they were crocheted, even if I couldn't think of the Japanese term. But I didn't connect them to you."

"I was afraid of that," Mrs. Morton said warmly. "That's why I carried my paperback with me everywhere. I've read it twice over." Returning to her place, she rooted around in her bag until she came up with the novel Pauley had mentioned.

"Agatha Christie," Jem said. "*Sparkling Cyanide.* Right."

"Yes. I think that was a bit subtle as well. When you're a mastermind, you tend toward the subtle, but as I mentioned, if you want to make things sporting, you really must give the sleuth a fighting chance. If you could have seen my entry into the Bake Off, I reckon you would have put two and two together. But of course, it was my bad luck that Isolde's cake was served first, and my cake never got a showing."

"Was it shaped like a death's head?" Micki asked.

"Nothing so obvious." Mrs. Morton tittered. Either the stress of being revealed before everyone as a murderess had got to her, or she was simply enjoying herself too much to feign decorum. "It was a peach-infused cake topped with candied peach blossoms. Gorgeous. Some of my best work. I really hope now that this silly mass paranoia has been cleared up that everyone will try a slice. It would be criminal to let such a masterpiece go to waste. And it's perfectly delectable, I promise."

Rhys hooted. Everyone turned to stare.

"Sorry." He shrugged. "Struck me as funny, that's all."

"You really have lost your mind," Mrs. Jones told Mrs. Morton, tone thick with contempt. "Lemmy Beaglehole was loathsome, but that didn't give you the right to take his life."

"Yes, it did," Mrs. Morton said. "He never should have written those lies about my Trevor." To her grandson sitting handcuffed and gobsmacked, she added, "I realize you're a bit startled just at the moment. But when you think it through, you'll see I'm right."

"Gran. You murdered a man." Trevor shook his head. "And if not for you, Agnetha and Xavier would be alive."

"Mrs. Morton, you're under arrest," Hack said. "You do not have to say anything. But it may harm your defense if you do not mention when questioned something which you later rely on in court. Anything you do say may be given in evidence..."

She thrust out her bony wrists. "Handcuffs. Surely you aren't forgetting to snap on the silver bracelets?"

"Well, given your age and the unique situation in which we find ourselves, I didn't think it was necessary right at this moment, but... sure. Why not? I almost get the feeling," he added, fastening the cuffs, "you view this as what some people call a bucket list experience."

"Of course it is." Mrs. Morton gazed down at the handcuffs, pulling against them experimentally and looking delighted when they didn't budge. "When Lobelia dreamed up her scheme to ruin King Triton's, I realized how much fun it was, being in on something illicit. I started to think of ways I could get back at Isolde for being so horrible to Trev. Then Lemmy was named judge and it all fell into place. At first I was so careful, covering my tracks, making sure if anyone got the blame, it would be Xavier. Then I realized that if I got away with it scot-free, the whole caper would end in a fizzle. No one would reconstruct the trouble I went to. No one would ever guess who the mastermind was. Of course, I thought the investigation would take days. I didn't reckon on being stuck here overnight with the Scilly Sleuth herself. It was all over so fast," she added a bit sadly. "But it was fun. Brilliant fun. Come here, love."

Jem blinked at the old lady. "Me?"

"Who else? Don't tell me you're afraid of me. I'm handcuffed, aren't I?"

An image of Hannibal Lecter, handcuffed and using his teeth to monstrous effect, came unbidden into Jem's mind. But she didn't really believe Mrs. Morton was reeling her in for one final *Silence of the Lambs* moment. At least not the bloody kind. After all, Anthony Hopkins's Hannibal had shown a genuine fondness for Jodie Foster's Clarice.

"What?" she asked, approaching cautiously.

"Closer."

Biting her lip, Jem tilted her ear toward Mrs. Morton. The old lady whispered a few words, then pulled back.

"All right, Sergeant Hackman. I'm sure you've devised

some humane but inescapable form of imprisonment to keep me on ice until the storm breaks. Take me away."

Still looking slightly overwhelmed by his strangely giddy confessed murderess, Hack led her away. Possibly to a broom closet, but more likely to someplace better ventilated, like the library. He'd be obliged to spend the rest of the waning night with her, even escorting her to the lavatory if she needed it, unless a woman from the assembled crowd offered to help out. Judging from the faces around the room, no one wanted anything more to do with Vera Lynn Morton, including her grandson.

"What did she say to you?" Pauley demanded.

"I thought I might have to drag her off you," Rhys said.

"Yeah, girl. Haven't you seen *Silence of the Lambs*? She could've bitten your face off. Or eaten you with fava beans and a nice Chianti." Micki imitated Hannibal's tongue-flicking hiss.

"She's that doolally," Fernsby agreed, shuddering. "What did she say?"

For Jem, that whispered declaration had been the candied peach blossom on top of the cake—a window into a psyche that took a hard turn somewhere and never returned. She didn't feel like discussing it with the room at large.

"Nothing much," she lied. "She just said sorry. Things got out of hand."

"I'll say they did." Keir stuck out his chin, pugnacious. "I was slandered. Some of you"—he looked significantly at Mrs. Jones and Trevor—"will be hearing from my solicitor."

"You'll have to pay him first," Mrs. Jones snapped. "Get down to the track and bet whatever you have left on a dark horse."

Rhys hooted again. This time he didn't apologize, and several others joined in.

"C'mon, Posh," Keir huffed, starting toward the lifts.

His wife didn't move.

"Posh! Move your arse."

"Move yours. I want a divorce."

To Jem's relief, that matrimonial grudge match soon exited Decant Resist. Both parties were sticking to their guns; Keir wanted a comprehensive apology, and Posh wanted out. Shouting and gesticulating all the way, they disappeared into a lift, removing their misery from the public eye at long last.

"Just think. If she divorces him, she won't have to subsist on bean curd and sprouts anymore," Pauley said.

"Did you see the tragic mess their cake left on the wall?" Micki asked. "I'd sooner eat Mrs. Morton's peach blossom murder cake. At least it would taste good going down."

"I'm pretty sure Keir has a blonde bit of stuff stashed in Penzance," Rhys said. "Reckon I ought to let that slip to Posh?"

"Aces," Micki said approvingly.

"I'm not speaking to you," Pauley said.

"You're speaking to me, aren't you?" Pranav asked.

"Of course. You didn't mean any harm. You were drawn into his wicked ways. It could happen to anyone," Pauley said reassuringly.

"Fine." Rhys turned to Jem. "I suppose you're still cross with me, too?"

Jem shook her head. "I could pretend to be. But when Xavier got struck, all I could think of was it might have been you. You shouldn't have run after him like that."

"I should have run faster," Rhys countered. "Then I

might have dragged him back to safety in time, and we could have interrogated him, and solving this mess would have been easier."

"You just have to be the hero, don't you?"

He shrugged. "You're the one who always solves the mystery. I'm just the muscle."

Something about that bit of great British self-deprecation made Jem want to kiss him. And so, she did.

23

AN ARREST, A JOB OFFER, AND A RING POP

"But everyone was so desperate to leave when it was impossible," Jem said, looking around the Bay View's common room. It was packed to the gills. Jem saw once-stranded guests, random employees, most of the kitchen staff, two junior detectives from Devon & Cornwall, and the entire Isles of Scilly police force, who'd turned out partly to see the murderer apprehended, and partly to reassure themselves that Hack was okay.

Watching PC Newt and the others take turns punching his arm, or accusing him of attention-seeking, and so on, gave Jem a warm feeling. It had taken awhile, but the IoS constabulary had fully accepted their new boss. Judging by Hack's poorly feigned annoyance, he was enjoying himself. Maybe he'd never get back to a metropolitan beat like Exeter, but working in paradise had its own rewards. Plus, statistically more murders than anyone now cared to talk about.

Naturally, when the mainland murder squad arrived, DS Conrad had come with them, clinging on to power in his final weeks before mandatory retirement. But while the senior detectives had immediately converged on Mrs. Morton, Trevor, Isolde, and Mrs. Jones, commandeering the ballrooms to do preliminary interviews, Conrad had barely shown his face inside Bay View, preferring to stalk around the rain-drenched lawn as if personally digging up over-looked clues. Through the big picture window, Jem saw a reporter with a microphone and a cameraman asking him questions. It was a perfect shot—storm-ravaged landscape, downed tree limbs, flooded meadows, a faint rainbow, and DS Conrad, looking like a crime-solving chiffonier in a trench coat.

Stay out there, she thought at him, full of cheerful malice. *Don't even think about coming in here to growl at me and my ragtag accomplices, or I'll laugh in your big clay face.*

Micki appeared, pushing her way through the crowd to where Jem, Pauley, and Rhys stood, backed up against the check-in desk. Static crowds made her restless, so she'd slipped outside to assess the scene.

"Pranav's helicopter isn't back yet. But there are three ferries out at the quay, still mostly empty," Micki said. "I can't believe after all the whinging and bleating about being stuck here, these people are still hanging around."

"It's the perp walk," Rhys declared. "Everybody wants to see the Mad Poisoner frogmarched off to justice." He poked Pauley, who started a little but refused to turn around. "Hey. Is that what you want? For Hack to cuff me and parade me around as a bad friend?"

"It would be a start. I can't believe you followed me. *Stalker.*"

"I can't believe you lied to me. *Felix Catchpole.*"

"I lied to you because you can't handle the truth."

"I can't handle the truth because you're too good for

every gormless git you've ever dated. Except now. Pranav's all right. I admit it."

"Big of you," Pauley scoffed, still not turning around.

Rhys poked her again. Whirling, Pauley made a grab for his poking finger. Soon they were dodging and poking their way into the potted alocasia dawn, which shivered all over as an especially well-aimed poke sent Rhys stumbling into it.

"You and him need to get back on track, and that's just the way to do it," Micki murmured to Jem. "A wild poke session. I mean—that came out wrong. Then again..." She shrugged, smiling.

Before Jem could formulate a clever reply, an *ohh* sound rippled through the room, starting near the lifts and widening like pond ripples to encompass the entire crowd. As perp walks went, it was curiously unsatisfying, because the arresting officers were all at least six feet tall. Flanking Mrs. Morton on either side, they effectively shielded the old lady from view while crossing to the exit. As the foremost copper opened the door, a break in the bodies suddenly revealed Mrs. Morton, crocheted cap on her head and hand-cuffs locked around her wrists. With uncanny accuracy, she looked over her shoulder and found Jem standing by the check-in desk. Their eyes met. It was fleeting, the briefest of connections, but unforgettable.

"Did that little psycho just wink at you?" Micki spluttered.

"When she said my sleuthing made her day, I think she meant it," Jem said.

Pauley and Rhys, who'd paused their pokefest to observe the perp walk with all due solemnity, seemed to have put aside their mutual snit.

"Look at poor Mrs. Jones," Pauley said, noting Mrs.

Morton's lifelong friend, who was exiting the second lift in the company of Isolde and Trevor. "She's gobsmacked. Trev and Isolde look better than expected, frankly." In a lower voice she added, "Her hand is on his shoulder. Is that friendship? Or something else?"

"Pretty funny if dear old grandmum's scheme to get Isolde out of the picture ends with them getting remarried," Micki said.

"Jemmie." Rhys leaned close. "I've been meaning to ask. What did Mrs. Morton whisper to you after you solved the case?"

"Oh, that." Jem sighed. "She said, 'Not everyone can be a sleuth. But everybody can be a murderer if they only put their mind to it.'"

"Barking," Micki said.

"Doolally," Pauley said.

"Correct," Rhys said. "But barmy, obviously. Jemmie, follow me. I found something you might want a look at."

"Does it involve getting away from this crowd?"

"Yes."

"Perfect." Jem had followed Rhys several yards when she realized Micki and Pauley had stayed put. Micki smiled and waved. Pauley was clutching both hands together as if on the verge of something wonderful.

"What's got into them?"

"Nothing. C'mon."

He led her past the ballrooms, through the kitchen, and into the cloakroom. There, his dog-smelling plaid mac hung on its peg, looking like an advert for painless euthanasia. As he rifled through the coat's pockets, Jem's mobile shocked her by chirruping. This first notification was followed by a volley of identical electronic pings. It was a relief to be connected again. And kind of sad to feel the digital ball and chain snap around her ankle once more.

"Jemmie..."

"Just a sec." Scrolling rapidly through her notifications, she was both pleased and astonished to find a curt, to-the-point email from Minting, reframing their conversation in Kestrel & Peregrine as a job proposal. So it hadn't been just a temporary overflow of gratitude over the insulin. He was creating a new post for her at the Courtney, overseeing his pet project, "Cornwall: The Fifth Nation." She would be doing what she loved again—and answering to someone who valued her occasional escapades as the Scilly Sleuth. Of course, she'd occasionally have to rub shoulders with her former boss, the prickly Mr. Atherton. But if he could endure it, she could.

"I'm hired," she cried, looking up from her screen at last. But Rhys was no longer standing by his horrible plaid mac. He was kneeling on the tile floor, offering something up to her.

"What is that?" she heard herself mutter.

"London blue. Two hundred carats. Cut in the... er, pacifier style." Rhys was grinning, but his eyes were serious. And hopeful. "Try it on."

Scoffing, Jem accepted the novelty ring. It was the kind from the Bay View's gift shop. The candy those free-range kids had been rowing over.

"Fits," Jem said. Of course it did. The plastic ring was open so it could snap on a finger of any size, even a grown-up one.

"Perfect. Marry me."

"That isn't a question."

"You might say no to a question."

"Rhys..."

He sprang up, taking her left hand with its bulbous candy gemstone and brushing his lips against her fingertips. She shivered. Playing the Pransome Hense in that comedy must have given him a few pointers in the romantic gesture department.

"Look. I can't afford a real ring. The cottage is still— well. Suboptimal. I've never lived with anyone before and I'm sure to get some yellow cards. But you're no paragon. Yesterday, you were completely mental—"

"This is like a *Pride and Prejudice* proposal. One of the insulting ones."

"The point is, we belong together. We've fought our whole lives. We're not going to stop rowing just because we're in love. So marry me and that way, the next time you storm out in the middle of a, well, storm, I won't have to risk my neck following you in a helicopter to say sorry."

Jem drew in a deep breath. "Admit you dumped Buck's doggy toys on the bed just to infuriate me."

"Admit you ran away to Pauley's because you knew you were more wrong than right."

She blew out a sigh. He did the same. Not to imitate her, but because they were perfectly in sync.

"You drive me nuts."

He grinned.

"Not a compliment!"

"I know. Marry me, Stargazer."

"Fine."

"Is that a yes?"

She held back her answer as long as she could stand it, staring hard into his triumphant blue eyes. "Yes," she burst out at last, and he kissed her. Most of her brain was occupied with the kiss. But a tiny part registered what sounded like a suppressed cheer from just outside the cloakroom.

Pulling back, she asked, "Did Pauley and Micki follow us?"

"Probably. What did Keir call them?"

"My ragtag gang of accomplices. Don't smirk. He meant you, too. Hey—did we just get engaged on the fifteenth of February?"

"Yep."

"But nobody gets engaged on the day after Valentine's Day."

"Maybe not," he said. "But it suits us, don't you think?"

Jem thought a moment and decided it did. Squeezing Rhys's hand, she popped her engagement ring in her mouth —it tasted like blue raspberry—and went forth to share her happy news.

A LETTER FROM EMMA

Thank you so much for reading *A Death at Bay View Hotel*. If you would like to be informed of my future releases, please sign up at the following link. I love hearing from my readers and sharing writing news with them.

www.bookouture.com/emma-jameson

I always enjoy dreaming up adventures for Jem Jago and her friends, and in this novel, I tried something new for me: a variation of the locked room mystery. My favorite scene was Jem and Pauley out in the storm, searching for Jace's insulin. I've never written a scene quite like that, and by the end of the book, I felt as though Storm Veronica was a character too.

I also had fun paying off some dangling threads from previous books. Micki's back to singing in public, Pauley and Pranav seem well on their way—if they're using endearments like "honey bear" in public—and Rhys finally pops the question to Jem. Since *Pride and Prejudice* is one of my favorite books, Rhys, of course, went off the rails a bit in the course of his proposal—like Mr. Collins, whose proposal insulted Elizabeth Bennet somewhat, only to be outdone by Mr. Darcy, who insulted her quite thoroughly while declaring his love.

As I've mentioned before, it's nice to look back on how much Jem has grown since returning to Cornwall and the

Isles of Scilly. The Jem Jago we met on page one of *A Death at Seascape House* was rather closed-off, diffident, and lacking in a certain confidence. The Jem in this book is resilient, trusting of her friends, and quick to regroup and forgive. That's growth.

One last thing. If you enjoyed *A Death at Bay View Hotel*, please consider posting a review online. Honest reviews are literally priceless. They make all the difference in the life of a book. Thank you so much.

Cheers,

Emma Jameson

www.emmajamesonbooks.com

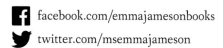 facebook.com/emmajamesonbooks
twitter.com/msemmajameson

ACKNOWLEDGMENTS

Working with Bookouture has been a wonderful experience, and I have so many people to thank. First, my helpful and especially encouraging editor, Kelsie Marsden. Her support has been indispensable. Second, my copyeditor, Jane Eastgate, who as always patiently corrects a multitude of sins.

I'd also like to mention Lisa Brewster, who designed this book's cover, and Tamsin Kennard, the voice of Jem and everyone else in my imaginary community, who performs the audiobook editions.

Thanks to the entire Bookouture team!